Beth Ellis

An English Girl's First Impression of Burmah

Beth Ellis

An English Girl's First Impression of Burmah

ISBN/EAN: 9783337227388

Printed in Europe, USA, Canada, Australia, Japan

Cover: Foto ©Andreas Hilbeck / pixelio.de

More available books at **www.hansebooks.com**

AN ENGLISH GIRL'S

FIRST IMPRESSIONS

OF

BURMAH.

BY

BETH ELLIS.

" "TIS TRUE 'TIS STRANGE, BUT TRUTH IS
ALWAYS STRANGE ; STRANGER SOME-
TIMES THAN FICTION."

Wigan :
R. PLATT, 17, WALLGATE.
London :
SIMPKIN, MARSHALL, HAMILTON, KENT & CO., LTD.
1899.

DEDICATED

T. E.

ILLUSTRATIONS.

—

CONTENTS.

INTRODUCTION.

———

Towards the close of my visit to Burmah I was dining one night at a friend's house in Rangoon, when my neighbour, a noted member of the I. C. S. suddenly turned to me and asked me if it was my intention to write a book. At my prompt reply in the negative he seemed astonished, and asked, what then did I intend to do with my life? I had never looked at the matter in that light before, and felt depressed. It has always been my ambition to do at Rome as the Romans do, and if, as my questioner clearly intimated, it was the custom for every casual visitor to the Land of Pagodas either to write a book or to "do something with his life," my duty seemed clear. I had no desire at all to undertake either of the tasks, but as there was apparently no third course open to me, I decided to choose the safer of the two, and write a book. So far so good, but what to write about? I have considered the merits of innumerable subjects, from the exploits of the old Greek heroes to green Carnations, but each appears to have been appropriated by some earlier author. The only subject which, so far as I can discover, has never hitherto formed the theme of song or story, is Myself, and as that is a subject about which I ought to know more than most folks and which has always appeared to me to be intensely interesting, I have adopted it as the theme of this, my first plunge into Literature.

CHAPTER I.

THE VOYAGE.

"Who spoke of things beyond my knowledge and showed
me many things I had never seen before."

"For to admire, and for to see, and for to behold
the world so wide."—(Rudyard Kipling.)

"I AM not naturally a coward, except when I am afraid; at other times I am as brave as a lion."

It is an unfortunate state of existence, but such it is. From my babyhood I have been known to my friends and relations as one who might be confidently expected to behave in a most terror-stricken manner on all occasions when no real danger threatened; but for myself, I have always felt convinced that should I ever be brought face to face with real danger, I should behave with a coolness and courage calculated to win the unbounded admiration of all beholders. I say advisedly "of all beholders," because, possibly, were no witnesses present, I might not feel disposed to show so resolute a front to the danger!

A

For example, in the case of a shipwreck, I can picture myself presenting my life-belt to any one in distress, in the most self-sacrificing manner, with the neatest little speech, quite worthy of "Sir Philip Sidney" himself, and from some commanding post of vantage in the rigging, haranguing the terrified passengers on the advisability of keeping their heads. I feel sure that no power on earth would prevent me from diving into the raging sea to rescue inexpert swimmers from a watery death, were such an opportunity to present itself to me.

And yet, if I am taken out of my depth, during a morning bathe, I am paralysed with fear. Though a brave and expert swimmer in shallow water, no sooner do I find myself out of reach of dry land, than all my powers forsake me. I swim with short, irregular, and utterly in-effective strokes, I pant, gasp and struggle, and unless promptly rescued, I sink.

Or again, I can in imagination picture myself snatching little children from under the hoofs of maddened horses, or with a plunge at the reins, stopping them in the full force of their desperate career.

But in reality I have never yet had sufficient courage to enter into close intimacy with any horse, maddened or otherwise. Once, when I wished to ingratiate myself in the eyes of the owner, I did venture to pat a horse gingerly on the neck, well out of reach of mouth or heels, but the animal shied away promptly, and I have never repeated the experiment.

Twice indeed, when a small girl, I was induced to mount to the saddle, and then my expectations were not disappointed. Real danger stared me in the face, and I was brave. When the horse, for some unaccountable reason, pricked its ears, tossed its head, and began to trot, I did not scream, I did not call for help, I merely grasped the pummel with one hand, the saddle with the other, shut my eyes and waited for the end. The end was sudden and somewhat painful.

But in this matter-of-fact little England of ours there are few opportunities, outside the yellow backed novel, of meeting with real adventures. Picture then my delight when I received an invitation to spend the winter in Burmah. I knew where Burmah was; that it was bounded by Siam, China, and Tibet; anything was possible in a country with such surroundings. I was charmed to go.

Accordingly, I bought a great many unnecessary things, as is ever the custom with inexperienced travellers, and started from Liverpool early in November, my mind filled with dreams of tiger shooting, cobra killing, dacoit hunting, and other venturesome deeds.

After I had recovered from the effects of homesickness, brought on by my first venture into the unknown world, and sea sickness brought on by the Bay of Biscay, I found the ship a world of hitherto undreamt of delights. I suppose the voyage was much the same as all other voyages, but to me, naturally, it was full of enjoyments, wonders, and new experiences. Everything was delightful, including the "Amusement Committee" and "Baggage

Days"; even coaling, I think, for the first five minutes was full of interest.

I have since been told that my fellow passengers were not uncommon types, but to me they appeared the most wonderful and interesting beings who ever lived in this work-a-day world. Certainly, none could have been kinder to a lone, lorn female than were they. There were, of course, on board several other passengers making their first voyage, young Indian Civilians much advised and patronised by seniors of two years standing, but these were of interest only as partners in games and dances. It was in the real seasoned article, the self-satisfied, and immensely kind-hearted Anglo-Indian, in whom I found my real interest.

And they were all very good to me. Finding me young, ignorant, and eager for information, they undertook my education, and taught me many things which I did not know before, shedding new light on all subjects, from "the only way to eat a banana," to the object of creation.

I learned that India was created that the Indian Civilian might dwell therein ; the rest of mankind was created in order to admire the Indian Civilian. Something of this sort I had already heard from my brother-in-law, a member of that service, but one does not pay much attention to what brothers-in-law say.

Burmah, I discovered, is a land where teak grows, in order that the "Bombay Burman" may go there and collect it. I have no very clear idea as to what this "Bombay Burman" may be, but suppose him to be a member of a society of men who uphold the principles of a late Prime Minister; not political, but woodcraft.

There are other dwellers in India and Burmah ; indeed, one man proved to me that the welfare of the British Constitution was solely dependent upon the efficient condition of the Burmese police force, of which he was an important member, but his arguments seemed to me a trifle involved. On the whole, the other inhabitants of these countries seem to be of little use or importance, unless perhaps it be to amuse and entertain the Indian Civilian and the "Bombay Burman" in his leisure hours.

Further, I was instructed that Ceylon is a country in which dwell the best (and the noisiest!) fellows in the world. They have innumerable horse races, eat prawn curry, are prodigiously hospitable, and in odd hours grow tea.

My fellow passengers also filled my eager mind with stories of wonderful adventure. Burmah, apparently, is crowded with tigers and wild elephants, of a size and ferocity which filled me with fear. But as every man on board appeared to have slain tigers and captured elephants innumerable, and that under the most surprisingly dangerous circumstances, I felt I should be well protected.

I was also taught how to overcome a wild beast, should I chance to meet with one when weaponless.

A bear should cause but little anxiety; it is only necessary to hit him violently over the nose; he will then stop and cry, and his victim will escape. But beware!

one man was so much amused at the bear's strange cry that he laughed and forgot to run away. The bear killed him.

When chased by an elephant the pursued should, I believe, climb up a clump of feathery bamboos, where the beast cannot reach him. When I saw a clump of feathery bamboos I rather wondered how anyone could climb it; but all things are possible to one pursued.

A tiger presents greater difficulties. If he doesn't run away when you wave your arms and shout, you should poke your stick through his eye into his brain, or get on his back, out of reach of his claws, and throttle him. If that fails, pretend to be dead; if that even fails, you must die.

All this information I accepted gratefully and stored in my memory for use when opportunity should arise. In the meantime I continued to enjoy my voyage, and turned all my energies to mastering the science of board-ship games.

The one game which I never could play was "Bull." To me it seemed the most foolish game ever invented. It is played by means of six flat pads, about two inches in diameter, and a large sloping black board, divided by thick white lines into twelve squares. Ten of these squares are marked with numbers, the remaining two with "Bs." The object of the player is to throw the pads on to the centre of the squares, avoiding the lines, which count nothing, and above all avoiding the "Bs," which count "minus ten." At the end of each turn the total of the numbers scored is reckoned, and the highest score wins.

In the "Bull" tournament I was drawn to play with a Mr. Rod, whom I did not know, but who enjoyed the reputation of being an excellent player, and very keen to win. One morning I was practising, and playing, if possible, worse than usual, when I noticed a melancholy-looking man, seated on a camp stool, watching my performance. I was struck by his ever increasing sadness of expression, and enquired his name.

He was Mr. Rod.

In the tournament my score was minus

twenty ; I did not see him any more during the voyage !

I learned that one or two people had seen a worse "Bull" player than myself. Her first three throws went overboard, the fourth went down an air funnel, and the fifth upset an ink-stand, showering the contents over an innocent spectator of the game. She never attempted to play "Bull" again ; it had made her so unpopular.

Great indeed are the attractions of board-ship life on a first voyage. The congenial companionship, the exhilarating outdoor life, the constant succession of games, gaieties, and amusements, the novelty of every thing, all tend to shed a halo over what, to the seasoned traveller, is merely a period of utter boredom, to be dragged through with as little ennui as possible. But the chief charm to me lay in the glimpse, though only distant, of new lands, lands which had hitherto been merely geographical or historical names, but which now acquired a new reality and interest.

The first few days we saw little of the land, but after the Bay was passed, our course lay more inland, and we saw the coast of Spain and Portugal, beautiful in the sunlight, red rocks and green slopes rising up from a sea of deepest blue.

Then appeared on the horizon a vague shadowy cloud, which we learned was Africa. The first glimpse of a new continent, and a continent fraught with such endless possibilities is impressive ; and as we drew nearer, and gazed on that dark range of wild, bare hills, I sympathised thoroughly with a wee fellow-passenger who was discovered, full of mingled hope and terror, looking eagerly at the dreary waste of land in search of lions !

Soon again we forgot all else, when, shaping our course round the south of Spain, Gibraltar broke upon our view. What a wonder it is ! that great rugged rock, shaped on the northwest like a crouching lion, rising dark, cold and solitary, amid the alien lands around it. Unmoved by the raging seas beneath, it stands calm and defiant, a fit emblem of the nation to which it belongs.   Surely no Englishman can behold Gibraltar without feeling proud of his nationality.

We passed close to the north of Corsica, where the hills were covered with snow, though it was still early winter. A dreary inhospitable looking country is this : a fit birthplace for that iron-heart the First Napoleon.

We passed through the Straits of Messina by full moonlight, and never have I beheld a scene of more fairylike beauty. The Sicilian coast seemed (for all was vague and shadowy) to rise in gentle slopes from the dark water, the land looked thickly wooded and well cultivated, and here and there appeared the little white towns, nestling among trees and vineyards, or perched beneath sheltering rocks, a peaceful and beautiful paradise. On the Italian coast the scenery was a complete contrast, the high, fierce hills stood up black and frowning against the clear sky, the country was wild, dreary and desolate. This mingling of peaceful homelike landscape, and weird rugged scenery, with the tender romance of the moon shining on the still dark water, reminded me, somehow, of Wagner's music ; nothing else can so fitly represent the scene.

Our course did not carry us very near to Crete, but we saw Mount Ida rising beautiful and snow-crowned in the centre of a tumultuous land. What scorn and pity this fair Mother Ida must feel for the miserable dwellers at her feet !

We stopped at Port Said for four hours. During the first two hours I was charmed with the place ; it seemed just like a big exhibition, everything was so strange and unreal. The donkeys were delightful, the Turkish traders so amusing, and shopping, when one has to bargain twenty minutes over every article, and then toss up about the price, is certainly a new experience.

During the third hour I found that the heat, dust, and endless noise and chatter were far from unreal. I had bought every conceivable thing that I could not possibly want, and paid three times the proper price for it. The Arabs ceased to be amusing ; I was bored to tears.

During the fourth hour I grew to hate the place and its inhabitants with a deadly hatred, and could have kissed the ship in my delight at returning to her, had she not been covered with coal dust.

My first experience of the natives of Port Said was a long brown arm coming through my porthole, feeling about for whatsoever valuable it might find ; a hearty smack with a hair brush caused it to retire abruptly. The last I saw of them was a pompous trader thrown overboard with all his wares, because he would not leave the ship when ordered. His companions in their boat, I noticed, busily rescued the wares, but seemed quite indifferent to the safety of the poor owner, whom they left to struggle to shore as best he could.

It is said that one would meet everyone sometime at Port Said if one waited long enough ; I would rather forego the meeting.

The Canal, I believe, is generally regarded as an unmitigated nuisance, and indeed, the slow progress and constant stoppages make the passage through it a little wearisome, but on a first voyage its shores are most interesting. On one side are several inland seas, and small collections of the most wretched and impossible looking habitations that human beings ever inhabited, with an occasional oasis of tall green palm trees. From the east bank the desert stretches away apparently into infinity.

I was disappointed in the desert, though I hardly know what I expected ; I suppose the very emptiness and immensity detract from its impressiveness ; the human eye and mind cannot grasp them. We saw several mirages and felt quite pleased with ourselves, though unconvinced that they were not really oases in the desert ; they were so very distinct.

Some of the glimpses of native life on the banks were very amusing. At one spot we met a camel, smiling the foolish irritating smile which is a camel's characteristic, speeding away at an inelegant trot, and distantly pursued by the owner and his friends ; alas ! we could not see the end of the race.   Camels, I was told, are unwearying beasts, so perhaps, like "Charley's Aunt" this one is still running.

We were greatly excited by one incident. A Dutch steamer passed us, and we noticed on the deck a very pretty girl, evidently very much admired by all the crew, and especially by one tall fine looking fellow who seemed on very good terms with her.   Shortly after the boat had passed, a small steam launch hove into sight, on board of which were several men, mostly Turkish officials. As they passed, the skipper of the launch shouted various questions, and we gathered that "Mademoiselle" had run away and they were in pursuit.   Whether it was an elopement or merely an escape from justice we never learned, but most of us adopted the former view, and hoped that the guilty steamer would be out of the canal and safe from pursuit, before the fussy little launch overtook it.

We had a gorgeous sunset that night in the canal.   The sky, every conceivable shade of yellow, violet and crimson, was reflected in the still waters of the canal and inland seas. The tall palm trees rose darkest green against the brilliant sky, while the sand of the desert glowed golden and salmon pink, fading in the distance to the palest green ; and all the colours were softened by a shadowy blue haze. I have never seen more wonderful colouring.

After passing Aden we steamed uninterruptedly for ten days with but occasional glimpses of land ; we had perfect weather, and the beauty of everything was almost overpowering.

I know not which hour of the day was the most exquisite : the early morning, with the sun rising, a ball of fire, out of the sea, making golden paths across the water, and the distant land blushing rosy red, as it peered through the hazy blue curtains which o'erhung it ; or the full noonday, with the deep blue sky and the deep blue sea fading together in a pale blue mist, till the world seems changed to a blue ball, and we the only living things within

B

it ; or the evening, when the western sky turned crimson and violet, and the sun, looking strangely oval, went down into the sea behind a transparent green haze, while in the east the crescent moon sailed silver in the blue-black sky ; or the night, when one lay alone on the upper deck, fanned by the soft night breeze, soothed by the monotonous swish of the water, looking into the unmeasured heights of the star-bespangled heavens or the impenetrable depths of the waters beneath, where "there is neither speech nor language: but their voices are heard among them," and the glory of God is shown forth night and day.

We had a fancy dress ball in the Red Sea : I suppose this is usual. Ours was noted for the number of Japanese present. At least, I believe they were intended to represent Japanese (the costumes had been bought at Port Said as such), but as they were dressed chiefly in European evening dress, partially covered by a flimsy Japanese dressing-gown, their appearance was unique.

I suffered a great deal on that occasion. I was a peasant, and as is the custom of fancy dress peasants all the world over, I wore my hair in a long plait down my back.

When my first partner approached I looked up at him in the usual polite and pleasing manner; he then seized my waist, plait included, in a firm grip and we danced off together, I with my head forcibly fixed at an angle such as is usually adopted by pictured good choir boys or "Souls awakening." I endured it for a short time; but then I began to get a stiff neck, and was obliged at last to ask my partner not to pull my hair. Alas! he was a sensitively shy youth, and was so embarrassed at my request that I felt I had committed an unpardonable fault.

But I did not learn by experience : the same thing occurred with all my partners, and as, after the first unfortunate attempt I did not like to complain again, the agonies I suffered from the crick in my neck next day can better be imagined than described.

We stayed two days in Ceylon, but all
attempts to describe this "Garden of
Eden" are futile. No one, who has not
seen it, can hope to realise the wonderful
colouring of the place ; the red roads, the
red and white houses, deep blue sky, and
deep blue lakes ; the brilliant dresses of
the natives, the large flaming red and
blue flowers, the wonderful green of the
palms and other tropical plants, and above
all, the beauty of that long line of open
coast, the great breakers glittering with a
thousand opal tints in the sunlight, and
beyond them the dark blue ocean, delicately flecked with shimmering white
spray, stretching away into the shadowy
distance, "farther than sight can follow,
farther than soul can reach."

We drove through the Cinnamon gardens, where the still air was heavy with
the delicious scent, and out to Mount
Lavinia, where, of course, we ate
prawn curry. Honestly, I must confess
that never before have I tasted anything
so truly horrible; but I pretended to like
it immensely. I suppose everybody does

the same when first introduced to this
celebrated dish : it is what might be called
" an accrued taste."

I don't think the author of " From
Greenland's Icy Mountains " can ever have
touched at Ceylon, or how could he have
declared that "man is vile"? The Singalese
are the most beautiful people I have ever
beheld, while the European inhabitants
are surely the most hospitable and delightful in the world.

Perhaps, when the poet wrote those lines,
he had the Turkish traders in his mind :
they certainly are vile. One of them sold
me a sixpenny bracelet for ten shillings.
They are exactly like the spider of noted
memory ; they stand at the doors of their
fascinating, dark, poky little shops, per-
suading innocent passers by to enter,
" only to look round ; " but if the poor
victim once venture to " walk into their
parlour," he will be indeed clever if he
escape without emptying his purse.

" Rickshaws " are charming ; I spent
every spare minute riding about in one.
It is almost as adventurous and exciting as

driving in a Marseilles Fiacre, and far more comfortable. I feared I had met with an adventure one day, for my "puller" (I don't know what else to call him) ran away with me, and stopping in a lonely road, began to assure me that I was a "handsome lady." I wondered what would happen next, but soon discovered that he only wanted "Backsheesh," and assuming my very sternest demeanour I repeated "don't bus" ("bus" to stop, being the only word of the language I could remember) several times, and at last induced him to take me back to my companions. What a valuable thing is presence of mind on such an occasion !

It was shortly after leaving Ceylon that our first real adventure befell us. We had all retired early to bed, being weary with the long day on shore ; the clatter of tongues and tramp of feet on deck had ceased, and all was silent save for the throbbing of the engines, and the quiet movements of the men on watch.

Suddenly I was awakened by a hurried murmur of voices in the next cabin, then an electric bell rang and I was terrified to hear the cry : " Fire ! Fire ! "

I sprang up, flung on a cloak, and rushed out into the "Alley Way," which speedily became the scene of the wildest confusion.

All the cabin doors opened, and the occupants hurried confusedly out, arrayed in the first garments that came to hand, asking eager questions, and giving wild explanations.

Brave men, anxious to be of use, snatched children from their mothers' arms, while the distracted mothers, having but a vague notion as to what was happening, supposed the boat to have been boarded by pirates or kidnappers, and fought fiercely to regain possession of their infants.

Those who prided themselves on their presence of mind, ran up and down with small water bottles to fling on the flames, or tried to organise a bucket line.   Others endeavoured to tie as many life-belts as possible to themselves and their friends, fastening them to any part of their persons most easily convenient.

One matter-of-fact old lady began to collect cloaks, biscuits, and valuables from her trunk, preparatory to being cast ashore on a desert island, while another proceeded to wrap herself from head to foot in blankets, having heard that these offer a good resistance to the spread of the flames. ̄ Some were too terrified to do aught but scream, but the majority were full of self-sacrifice and bravery, and fell over, and interfered with one another woefully, in their en-deavour to be of assistance to whomsoever might require their services.

Meanwhile the original causes of the alarm—two girls who shared the cabin next to mine—did not for an instant cease their efforts.   One, with a , fortitude worthy of Casabianca himself, stood firmly with a finger pressed upon the button of the electric bell, determined to die rather than leave her post, while the other fought her way wildly up the passage, turning a deaf ear to all ques-tions, and merely continuing to reiterate her cry of : "Fire ! Steward ! Fire !"

At length (I suppose, in reality, in about three minutes after the first alarm, but it seemed a far longer time) a sleepy and much astonished steward appeared, and as soon as he could make himself heard, demanded the cause of the uproar. When eagerly assured that the deck was on fire over our heads, that in five minutes we should all be cinders unless we instantly took to the boats, and that the whole affair was a disgrace to the Company, and the "Times" should be written to if the speaker (an irascible "Globe trotter") survived the disaster, the steward stolidly denied the existence of any fire at all and explanations ensued.

It was then discovered that signal rockets had been sent up from the deck to a signal station we were passing, and some of the sparks having blown into the porthole of the girls' cabin, the occupants had concluded that the deck was on fire, and had given the alarm.

It took some time to make the fact of the mistake clear to everyone, but the steward at last succeeded in

allaying all fears, and we returned to
our cabins, feeling indignant and somewhat foolish, and perhaps a little disappointed (now that the danger was
over) that our adventure had turned out
so tamely.

On the following morning the Captain
organised an imposing ceremony on the
upper deck, and solemnly presented two
sham medals to the heroines of the
preceding night's adventure, thanking
them for their presence of mind, and
noble efforts to save the burning ship !

The remainder of the voyage passed
without incident, and we arrived safely at
our destination about six o'clock one lovely
Friday morning. The sun was just rising
as we sailed up the river, tinting the brown
water and the green banks of the Irrawaddy with a rosy light. Rangoon, a
vast collection of brown and white houses,
mills, towers, chimneys, and cupolas, in
a nest of green, showed faintly through
the blue haze ; and rising high above a
grove of waving dark green palm trees,
glittered the golden dome of a pagoda,

the first object clearly distinguishable on shore, to welcome us to this country so rightly termed "The Land of Pagodas."

Chapter II.

RANGOON.

"Oh! the Land of Pagodas and Paddy fields green,
Is Burmah, dear Burmah you know."

This is not a book on "Burmah," but an account of my impressions of Burmah; therefore, for all matters concerning which I had no original impressions, such as its history, its public buildings, the scenery, the life and condition of the natives, its resources, and its future, I refer both the gentle and ungentle reader to the many books on the subject which have appeared during the past few years.

My first and last impression of Rangoon was heat. Not ordinary honest, hot, heat, such as one meets with at Marseilles or in the heart of the desert, wherever that may be; not even a stuffy heat, such as one encounters in church, but a damp, clinging, unstable sort of heat, which makes one long for a bath, if it were not too much trouble to get into it.

・ I remember in my youth placing one of my sister's wax dolls (mine were all wooden, as I was of a destructive nature) to sit before the fire one cold winter's day ; I remember dollie was somewhat disfigured ever afterwards.

The remembrance of that doll haunted me during my stay in Rangoon ; I felt I could deeply sympathise with, and thoroughly understand her feelings on that occasion ; and for the first two or three hours, remembering the effect the heat had upon her appearance, I found myself frequently feeling my features to discover whether they still retained their original form and beauty. But after a few hours I became resigned ; all I desired was to melt away quickly and quietly, and have done with it.

At first I looked upon the "Punkah" as a nuisance, its unceasing movement irritated me, it ruffled my hair, and I invariably bumped my head against it on rising. But after enduring one long Punkahless half-hour, I came to look on it as the one thing that made life bearable, and the

" Punkah-wallah " as the greatest bene-
factor of mankind.

In the early mornings and evenings I
became, hardly cooler, but what might be
described as firmer, and it was at these
times that the wonderful sights of Rangoon were displayed to my admiring gaze.

I saw the celebrated "Schwee Dagon
Pagoda" with its magnificent towering
golden dome, surmounted by the beautiful
gold and jewelled "Htee ;" the innumerable shrines, images, cupolas, and pagodas
at its base, the curious mixture of tawdry
decorations and wonderful wood carvings
everywhere visible, and the exquisite blending and intermingling of colours in the
bright dresses of the natives, who crowd
daily to offer their gifts at this most holy
shrine.   It is quite futile to attempt description of such a place ; words cannot
depict form and colour satisfactorily,
least of all convey to those who have not
themselves beheld it, a conception of the
imposing beauty of this world famed
Pagoda.

The Burmese are a most devout people ; the great flight of steps leading to the Pagoda is worn by the tread of many feet, and every day the place is crowded with worshippers.

They begin young. I saw one wee baby, scarcely more than a year old, brought by his father to learn to make his offering at the shrine of Buddha. The father with difficulty balanced the little fellow in a kneeling position before a shrine, with the tiny brown hands raised in a supplicating attitude, and then retired a few steps to watch. Instantly the baby overbalanced and toppled forward on its face. He was picked up and placed in his former position, only to tumble down again when left. This performance was repeated about five times ; the father never seemed to notice the humour of the situation—the baby certainly did not.

One of the most interesting sights of Rangoon is that of the elephants. Ostensibly their work is to pile timber ready for embarkation on the river, but evidently they consider that they exist and work in

order to be admired by all who pay them.
a visit.

And well they deserve admiration !
They go about their duties in a stately,
leisurely manner, lifting the logs with
trunk, tusks, and forefeet ; piling them up
with a push here, a pull there, and then
marching to the end of the pile and
contemplating the result with their heads
on one side, to see if all are straight and
firm.   And they do all in such a stately,
royal manner, that they give an air of
dignity to the menial work, and one
comes away with the feeling that to pile
teak side by side with an elephant would
be an honour worth living for.

During my peregrinations round the
town I was taken to see the home of the
Indian Civilian, a huge imposing building,
with such an air of awe-inspiring importance about every stick and stone, that
none save those initiated into the secrets
of the place, may enter without feeling
deeply honoured by the permission to do
so.   Even a " Bombay Burman " could
hardly approach, without losing some of
his natural hardihood.

ELEPHANT MOVING TIMBER

It may have been the awe with which this building inspired me, it may have been my visit to the Pagoda, with its air of mysticism and unknown possibilities, but when I retired to my large dimly lighted bed-room after my first day's wanderings in Rangoon, my natural courage forsook me, and I became the prey to a fit of appalling terrors.

All the ghostly stories I had ever read of the spiritualism of the East, of the mystic powers of "Thugs," "Vampires" and other unpleasant beings, returned to my mind.

For some time I could not sleep, and when at last I did sink into an uneasy doze I was haunted by nightmares of ghostly apparitions, and powerful and revengeful images of Gaudama.

Suddenly I awoke with the feeling that something, I knew not what, had roused me from my uneasy slumber. And then, as I lay trembling and listening, out of darkness came a Voice, weird, uncanny, which exclaimed in solemn tones the mystic word "Tuctoo."

What could it be?   Was I one destined
to learn deep secrets of the mystic world?
Had the spirit, if spirit it were, some
great truth to make known to me? if so,
what a pity it did not speak English!

"Tuctoo" remarked the voice again, this
time rather impatiently.

I racked my brains to think of a possible
meaning for this mysterious word, but
all in vain, I could understand nothing.

"Tuctoo, tuctoo, tuctoo" it continued.

And then, out of the darkness came
another voice, an angry English voice,
loud in its righteous indignation, the
voice of my host.

"Shut up you beast," he cried, and
perhaps he added one or two more words
suited to the occasion. I lay down and tried
to pretend that I had not been frightened,
and in doing so, fell asleep. I was introduced to the "Tuctoo" next day, but did
not consider him a pleasant acquaintance.
He is a lizard about a foot long, with a
large red mouth, and a long wriggling tail;
he reminded me of a baby alligator.   He
dwells on the inner walls of houses, and his

presence in a house is supposed to bring good luck, but his tiresome habit of "tuctooing" in a most human voice at all hours of the day or night make him rather unpopular. We chased him down the wall with a long "Shan" spear and caught him in a towel, but he looked so very pugnacious that we did not detain him from his business.

Of course the most important element of life in Rangoon, in fact in all Burmah, is the Gymkhana.

Apparently, the European population in Rangoon exists solely in order to go to the Gymkhana. It attracts like a magnet. People may not intend to go there when they set out, but no matter how far afield they go, sooner or later in the evening they are bound to appear at the Gymkhana. If they did not go there in the daytime they would inevitably walk there in their sleep.

This renowned Gymkhana is situate in the Halpin Road (pronounced "Hairpin," which is confusing to the uninitiated) and is a large, open, much verandaed, wooden building. Of the lower story, sacred to the male sex, I caught only a hurried glimpse in passing, and the impression left on my mind was a confusion of long men, reclining in long chairs, with long drinks.

On my first visit to the upper regions, I fancied myself in a private lunatic asylum, for there, in a large room built for the purpose, were numbers of men and women, to all other appearances perfectly sane, waltzing round and round to the inspiriting music of the military band ; dancing, in ordinary afternoon attire, not languidly, but vigorously and enthusiastically, and that in a temperature such as Shadrach, Meshech and Abednego never dreamed of.

But I soon discovered that there was method in this madness, for the heat, when dancing, was so unspeakably awful that to sit still seemed quite cool in contrast, and it was worth the sufferings of the dance to feel cool afterwards, if only in imagination.

In another room of the Gymkhana the ladies assemble to read their favourite magazines, or to glower from afar upon the early birds who have already appropriated them.

And here I must pause to say a word in deprecation of the accusations of gossip and scandal, which are so frequently launched against the Anglo-Indian ladies. Not that I would for the world deny the existence of scandal, but what I wish to emphasise is, that the Anglo-Indians (at least those of the female sex) do not invent or repeat scandalous stories from pure love of the thing, nor from any desire to injure the characters of their neighbours. They are forced to do so by circumstances.

For example, Mrs. A. arrives early at the Gymkhana, appropriates the newly arrived number of the "Gentlewoman," and seating herself comfortably in a good light, sets to work to read the paper from beginning to end.

But soon Mrs. B. appears upon the scene, and alas! Mrs. B. has also come to the Gymkhana with the intention of reading from beginning to end the newly arrived number of the "Gentlewoman"; and, being human, Mrs. B., on finding her favourite paper already appropriated, is filled with a distaste for all other papers, and a consuming desire to read "The Gentlewoman," and "The Gentlewoman" only. If she cannot procure the paper right speedily, life holds no more happiness for her.

But alas, Mrs. A. shows no intention of relinquishing her possession of the paper for many hours. In vain does Mrs. B. spread "Punch," "Graphic," or "Sketch," temptingly before Mrs. A's abstracted eyes, she is not to be influenced by honest means. Then Mrs. B. has only one course left to her, and adopts it.

First she seeks and obtains an assistant to the scheme, Mrs. C. The two ladies then draw near Mrs. A. (who tightens her hold on the paper as they approach) and seat themselves on either side of their victim.

Mrs. C., assuming an expression of sweet innocence, entirely disguising the craft of her intentions, pretends to be deeply interested in last week's "Gazette," hoping thereby to demonstrate her lack of interest in fashion papers; Mrs. B. entices Mrs. A. into conversation.

After a few desultory remarks, during which the aggressor still clings to her prey, Mrs. B., throwing a warning glance at Mrs. C. to prepare her, says in a voice fraught with deep mystery :

" Were you not astonished to hear of so and so's engagement last week ? "

No, Mrs. A. was not particularly astonished.

But surely Mrs. A. had heard that strange story about so and so's behaviour towards somebody else ?

Curious, Mrs. A. had not heard of it.

Of course Mrs. B. would not mention it to anyone else, but Mrs. A., as every one knows, can be trusted, and really it was so strange.

Then calling to her aid all her powers of imagination, Mrs. B. proceeds to relate some astounding invention concerning so and so. Gradually, as she becomes more interested in the recital, Mrs. A's. fingers relax their hold on the precious paper, and at last it is dropped, forgotten, upon the table.

Now it is Mrs. C's. turn. In the most careless manner she draws the "Gentle-woman" slowly towards her, until it is out of reach of Mrs. A., when she snatches it up eagerly, and retires to another table, where she is soon joined by the triumphant Mrs. B.

Then poor Mrs. A., deprived of her newspaper must needs seek another one, but alas? they are all in use. Nothing remains for her to do but to imitate Mrs. B's conduct, and attract Mrs. D's attention from the paper she is reading, by repeating to her the story she has just heard, adding whatever new details may appear to her as most likely to arouse Mrs. D's. interest. And so the snowball grows.

Thus it will be clear to all that the accusations are unfair, seeing that the gossip indulged in by the ladies at the Gymkhana is merely the outcome of circumstances, inventions being notoriously the children of necessity. It is obvious that were each lady in Burmah provided with every magazine and paper that her heart could desire, gossip would speedily cease to exist,—in the Ladies' Clubs.

The most extraordinary vehicle that ever existed is the Rangoon "ticca gharry." For inconvenience, discomfort, and danger, it has never been surpassed. It has been excellently described as "a wooden packing case on wheels." I suppose it is a distant and unfashionable relation of the modern four wheeler, with wooden shutters in place of windows ; very narrow, noisy, and uncomfortable. It is usually drawn by a long-tailed, ungroomed and brainless Burman pony, and is driven by one of the most extraordinary race of men that ever existed.

The "Gharry Wallah's" appearance— but it is scarce meet to describe his appearance to the gentle reader ; we will say his appearance is unusual. His mind and character have gained him his well earned right to be counted among the eccentricities of the age. He is sublime in his utter indifference to the world at large, in the cheerful manner in which he will drive, through, into, or over anything he happens to meet.

But his most noted characteristic is

utter indifference to the wishes of his "fare."

I have often wondered what are the secret workings of the "Gharry Wallah's" mind. He cannot imagine, (no man, intelligent or otherwise, could imagine) that a human being drives in a "gharry" for the pure enjoyment of the thing ; and yet he never seems to consider that his "fare" may desire to go to any particular destination. 'Tis vain to explain at great length, and with many forcible gestures, where one wishes to go ; "he hears but heeds it not." The instant one enters the vehicle he begins to drive at a great rate in whatever direction first comes into his mind. He continues to drive in that direction until stopped, when he cheerfully turns round and drives another way, any way but the right one.

No one has yet discovered where he would eventually drive to ; many have had the curiosity but none the fortitude to undertake original research into the matter.

It is presumed that, unless stopped, he would drive straight on till he died of starvation.

Occasionally, by a judicious waving of umbrellas it may be possible to direct his course, but that only in the case of a very young driver. I have sometimes wondered whether perchance the pony may be the sinner, and the driver merely an innocent and unwilling accomplice. I cannot tell.

But this I can say, if you crave for danger, if you seek penance, drive in a "ticca gharry," but if you desire to reach any particular destination in this century, don't.

With the exception of a few leisure hours spent at the Gymkhana, the ladies of Rangoon devote their time and energy to writing "Chits."

At first I was filled with a great wonder as to what might be the nature of these mysterious "Chits." I would be sitting peacefully talking with my hostess in the morning, when suddenly, a look of supreme unrest and anxiety comes over her face : "Excuse me, a moment" she exclaims, "I must just go and write a chit."

She then hastens to her writing table, rapidly scribbles a few words, gives the paper to a servant, and then returns to me with an expression of relief and contentment.

But scarce five minutes have elapsed, ere the look of anxiety again returns ; again she writes a "chit," and again becomes relieved and cheerful, and so on throughout the day.

And this, I discovered was the case with nearly every European lady in the country. I suppose it must be some malady engendered by the climate, only to be relieved by the incessant inditing of "chits." I myself never suffered from the ailment, but should doubtless have fallen a victim had I remained longer in the country.

The contents and destination of these "chits" seem to be of little or no importance ; so long as notes be written and despatched at intervals of ten minutes or so during the day, that is sufficient. What finally becomes of these "chits" I cannot pretend to say ; whether they are merely taken away and burnt, or whether they have some place in the scheme of creation, I never discovered.

Nor do I know whether the male population suffers from the same malady. Does the Indian Civilian, seated in his luxurious chamber in that awe-inspiring building of his, does he too spend his life in writing "chits"? Does the "Bombay Burman," in some far off jungle, "alone with nature undisturbed," does he too sit down 'neath the shade of the feathery bamboo, or the all embracing Peepul tree, and write and despatch "chits" to imaginary people, in imaginary houses, in an imaginary town?

I know not, it is futile to speculate further upon the matter. The mystery of "chit" writing is too deep for me.

I would gladly have remained longer in Rangoon, but it might not be. Mine was no mere visit of pleasure; I had travelled to Burmah in search of adventure, such as is scarcely to be met with in the garden party, dinner party, and dance life of Rangoon. And so, one hot afternoon, with anxious beating heart, I said "Good bye" to security and civilisation, and set forth on my journey to Mandalay!

Chapter III.

THE ROAD TO MANDALAY.

" I travelled among unknown men,
   In lands beyond the Sea."—(Wordsworth).
" Where the tints of the earth, and the hues of the sky,
In colour tho' varied, in beauty may vie."—(Byron).

THE distance by rail from Rangoon to Mandalay is 386 miles, and it takes twenty-two hours to accomplish the journey. Trains, like everything else in this leisurely country, are not given to hurrying themselves. "Hasti, hasti, always go hasti" is the motto for Burmah. As an example of the unintelligible nature of the language I may explain that "Hasti" means "slow !"

It is a pleasant journey however, for the carriages are most comfortable, and the scenery through which the rail passes affords plenty of interest to a new comer.

I enjoyed my journey, therefore, immensely. I left Rangoon about five o'clock in the afternoon, well provided with books, fruit and chocolates for the

journey, and under the protection of a
hideous Madrassee Ayah.

I believe she was in reality a worthy old
creature, but she was so exceedingly ugly,
so very unintelligible (though most persistent in her efforts at conversation) and
so intolerably stupid, that I could not feel
much affection for her, and I only consented to put up with her company as a
protection against the thieves who haunt
the various halting places along the line,
ready to steal into carriages and carry
away all the portable property of the
traveller. I had heard such blood curd-
ling stories of these train thieves that I
should have felt quite nervous about
undertaking the journey, had I not fortun-
ately disbelieved them.

I do not for an instant believe my ayah
would have been any real protection, for
whenever we stopped she was seized with
an overpowering hunger, and spent all her
time bargaining with the vendors of
bananas, huge red prawns, decayed fish,
dried fruits, cakes, and other horrible
articles, who swarmed upon the stations.

These delicacies, and others which she
prevailed upon my tender heart to buy for
her, she wrapped up in a large red pocket
handkerchief, and hid under the seat ;
what was their final fate I cannot pretend
to say, but for her sake I trust she didn't
eat them.

She was a much travelled lady and had
visited many of the towns along the route,
and persisted in waking me up at all odd
hours of the night, to point out the houses
where her various Mem-Sahibs had lived,
or the bungalows inhabited by the com-
missioners, matters in which I was not at
all interested.

She kept me awake with long rambling
stories about her many relations, stories
which, as they were told in the most
vague and unintelligible "pigeon English"
I found it very difficult to understand, but
the gist of all was that she was very
old and very poor, and she was sure I was
a very kind and generous " Missie," and
would not fail to reward her handsomely
for her services.

I failed to discover what these same

services might be, for beyond fanning me vigorously when I did not require it, and at three o'clock in the morning procuring me from somewhere an unpleasant mixture she called coffee, and which I was obliged to throw secretly out of the window, she did nothing except talk. I suppose she was really no worse than the rest of her tribe, and cannot be blamed for getting as much as she could out of her exceedingly inno-cent and easily humbugged " missie. "

At the first station at which we stopped, I was much astonished to see all the natives on the platform come and kneel down in the humblest manner round the door of my carriage, and remain there "shekkohing" and pouring forth polite speeches in Burmese, until our train left the station.

I have never been backward in my high opinion of my own importance, but I hardly expected the fame of my presence to have spread to this distant land, and felt considerably embarrassed, though, of course, highly gratified, by such unexpected tokens of respect.

D

I received these attentions at every station with the most royal bows and smiles, until at last, on dismounting from the train at the dining station, I discovered that the carriage next to mine was occupied by a noble Shan Chief and his retinue, and it was to him, not to my insignificant person, that all this homage was paid. I felt quite annoyed at the discovery. He was really such a hideous, yellow, dirty old man, and he sat at the window, surrounded by his wives and attendants, smoking grumpily, and paying not the least attention to the flattering speech of his admirers, who must have been far more gratified by my gracious condescension.

The chief stared at me a great deal when I passed his window to re-enter my carriage, and shortly after the train was again set in motion he sent one of his wives to inspect me, possibly with a view to offering me a position among the number of his dusky spouses. She opened the door, and stared at me for some time, taking not the slightest notice of my requests that she would withdraw, until she had sufficiently examined me, when she retired as abruptly as she had appeared, and I lost no time in securing the door behind her.

Evidently her report was not satisfactory, for I have heard no more of the episode. Possibly, she reported that I looked bad tempered ; I certainly felt so !

What a fascinating journey that was. During the first part of the route the country is less interesting, consisting merely of flat stretches of Paddy fields and low jungle scrub. But all this I passed through by night, when the soft moonlight lent a witching beauty to the scene.

There is something so inexplicably beautiful about night in the east, so comparatively cool, so clear, so quiet, and yet so full of mysterious sound,

"A little noiseless noise among the leaves,
Born of the very sigh that silence heaves."

The cloudless heavens sparkle with a myriad stars, the moonlight seems brighter and more golden than elsewhere, and the noisy, weary, worn old earth hides away

her tinsel shams and gaudiness, which
the cruel sunlight so pitilessly exposes, and
appears grander and nobler under night's
kindly sway.

The scenery in Upper Burmah is exceedingly fine. The great rocky hills, each
crowned with its pagoda, rise on all sides,
stretching away into the distance till they
become only blue shadows. Everywhere
are groves of bananas and palm trees,
forests of teak and bamboo, and vast
tracks of jungle, attired in the gayest
colours.

The pagodas, mostly in a half-ruined
condition, are far more numerous here
than in Lower Burmah, and raise their
white and golden heads from every towering cleft of rock, and every mossy grove.
As we neared Mandalay we passed many
groups of half-ruined shrines, images and
pagodas, covered with moss and creeper,
deserted by the human beings who
erected them, and visited now only by
the birds and other jungle folk, who build
their nests and make their homes in the
shade of the once gorgeous buildings.

They look very picturesque, rising above the tangled undergrowth that surrounds them, but pitifully lonely.

We stopped at a great number of stations en route. The platforms were always crowded with natives of every description, at all hours of the day and night, selling their wares, greeting their friends, or smoking contentedly, and viewing with complacency the busy scene.

The natives of India, with their fierce sullen faces, frightened me ; the cunning Chinese, ever ready to drive a hard bargain, amused but did not attract me ; but the merry, friendly little Burmese were a continual delight.

They swaggered up and down in their picturesque costumes, smoking their huge cheroots, the men regarding with self-satisfied and amused contempt the noisy chattering crowd of Madrassees and Chinese, the women coquetting in the most graceful and goodnatured way with everyone in turn. When they had paid their devoirs to the old chief, they would crowd round my carriage window offering their wares, taking either my consent or refusal to be a purchaser as the greatest joke, and laughing merrily at my vain attempts to understand them.

I fell in love with them on the spot, they are such jolly people and such thorough gentlefolk.

It was very interesting in the early morning to watch the signs of awakening life in the many Burmese villages through which we passed.   To see the caravans of bullock carts or mules setting out on their journey to the neighbouring town, and the pretty little Burmese girls coquetting with their admirers as they carried water from the well, or chattering and whispering merrily together as they performed their toilet by the stream, decking their hair with flowers and ribbons, and donning their delicately coloured pink and green " tamehns."

Here we met a procession of yellow-robed " hpoongyis " and their followers, marching through the village with their begging bowls, to give the villagers an opportunity of performing the meritorious duty of feeding them.   There a pro-

cession of men, women, and children
walking sedately towards a pagoda, with
offerings of fruit or flowers; to contem-
plate the image of the mighty Gaudama, to
hear the reading of the Word, and to medi-
tate upon the Holy Life.   Now we passed
a group of little hpoongyi pupils with
their shaven crowns and yellow robes,
sitting solemnly round their teacher in the
open-sided kyaung.   Anon we passed a
jovial crew of merrymakers in their most
brilliantly coloured costumes, jogging along
gaily behind their ambling bullocks, to
some Pwé or Pagoda Feast, which they
are already enjoying in anticipation.

And the strange part of it all is that
nowhere does one see sorrow, poverty, or
suffering; outwardly at least, all is bright
and happy.   I suppose the Burman must
have his troubles like other folk, but if so
he hides them extremely well under a
cheerful countenance.   Surely in no other
inhabited country could we travel so far
without beholding some sign of misery.

I think the great charm of Burmah lies
in the happiness and brightness of its

people ; their merriment is infectious, and they make others happy by the mere sight of their contentment.

We arrived at Mandalay about three o'clock in the afternoon. The last few hours of the journey were most unpleasantly hot, and I was very glad when we steamed into the station, and I saw my brother-in-law (who had descended from his "mountain heights" to meet me) waiting on the platform. The journey had been delightful in many ways, but after being twenty-two hours boxed up in a railway carriage with a chattering ayah, it was a great relief to reach one's destina-ation at last.

When I arrived in Mandalay I was filled with an overwhelming gratitude towards Mr. Rudyard Kipling for his poem on the subject.

Rangoon, fascinating and interesting though it be, is yet chiefly an Anglo-Indian town, but Mandalay, though the Palace and Throne room have been converted into a club, though its Pagodas and shrines have been dese-

-crated by the feet of the alien, and though
its bazaar has become a warehouse for
the sale of Birmingham and Manchester
imitations, yet, spite of all, this former
stronghold of the Kings of Burmah still
retains its ancient charm.

When first I experienced the fascination
of this wonderful town, my feelings were
too deep for expression, and I suffered as a
soda water bottle must suffer, until the
removal of the cork brings relief. Suddenly there flashed into my mind three
lines of Mr. Kipling's poem, and as I
wandered amid "them spicy garlic smells,
the sunshine and the palm trees and the
tinkly temple bells," I relieved my feelings
by repeating those wonderfully descriptive
lines ; I was once again happy, and I
vowed an eternal gratitude to the author.

Before the end of my two days stay in
Mandalay I began to look on him as my
bitterest foe, and to regard the publication
of that poem as a personal injury.

The Hotel in which we stayed was also
occupied by a party of American "Globe
Trotters." In all probability they were

delightful people, as are most of their
countrymen. They were immensely popular among the native hawkers, who
swarmed upon the door steps and ver-
andahs, and sold them Manchester silks
and glass rubies at enormous prices. But
we acquired a deeply rooted objection to
them, springing from their desire to live
up to their surroundings.

We should have forgiven them, had they
confined themselves to eating Eastern
fruits and curries, wearing flowing Burmese silken dressing gowns, and smatter-
ing their talk with Burmese and Hindustani
words. But these things did not satisfy
them. Evidently they believed that they
could only satisfactorily demonstrate their
complete association with their surroundings, by singing indefatigably, morning,
noon, and night, that most un-Burmese
song, " Mandalay."

They sang it hour after hour, during
the whole of the two days we spent
in the place.

In their bedrooms, and about the town
they hummed and whistled it, during

meals they quoted and recited it. At night,
and when we took our afternoon siesta,
they sang it boldly, accompanying one
another on the cracked piano, and all
joining in the chorus with a conscientious
heartiness that did them credit.

We tossed sleepless on our couches,
wearied to death of this endless refrain
that echoed through the house : or, if in
a pause between the verses we fell asleep
for a few seconds, it was only to dream of
a confused mixture of "Moulmein Pagodas," flying elephants, and fishes piling
teak, till we were once again awakened by
the uninteresting and eternally reiterated
information that "the dawn comes up like
thunder out of China 'cross the Bay."

The only relief we enjoyed, was that
afforded by one member of the party
who sang cheerfully : "On the Banks of
Mandalay," thereby displaying a vague-
ness of detail regarding the geographical
peculiarities of the place, which is so
frequently (though no doubt wrongly)
attributed to his nation.

And here I pause with the uncomfortable
feeling that in writing my experiences of

Burmah, I ought to make some attempt to describe this far-famed city of Mandalay, the wonders of its palaces, the richness of its pagodas, the brilliancy of its silk bazaar, and its other thousand charms.

But such a task is beyond me. Others may aspire to paint in glowing colours the fascinations of this royal town, and the beauty of the wonderful buildings ; but in my modesty I refrain, for to my great regret I saw little of them. My stay in the town was too short, and I was too weary after my journey, to admit of much sight-seeing. Beyond a short drive through the delightful eastern streets, and a hurried glimpse of the Throne Room, I saw nothing of the place, and the only thing I clearly recollect is the Moat, which I admired immensely, mistaking it for the far-famed Irrawaddy !

Therefore I will pass by Mandalay with that silent awe which we always extend to the Unknown, and leave it to cleverer pens than mine to depict its charms. "I cannot sing of that I do not know," especially nowadays when so many people *do* know, and are quite ready to tell one so.

CHAPTER IV.

THE JOURNEY TO THE HILLS.

"Old as the chicken that Kitmûtgars bring
Men at dâk bungalows,—old as the hills."
(Rudyard Kipling.)

The horse who never in that sort
Had handled been before,
What thing upon his back had got
Did wonder more and more.—"John Gilpin."

WE left Mandalay at half-past three in the morning, (our heavy baggage having preceded us in bullock carts the night before) and with our bedding and hand baggage packed with ourselves into a "ticca gharry," we started at that unearthly hour on our seventeen miles drive to the foot of the hills, where our ponies awaited us.

As we left the last lights of the town behind us, and drove out into the dreary looking country beyond, I was filled with a mixture of elation and alarm, but when my brother-in-law (I knew not whether seriously or in fun) remarked that he hoped we should meet no dacoits, the feeling of alarm predominated.

It would be an adventure, and I had come there purposely for adventure, but an adventure does not appear so fascinating in the dark at three o'clock in the morning, as it does at noonday. I was quite willing to have it postponed. However my companion seemed at home, and settled himself to sleep in his corner, so I endeavoured to do likewise.

But somehow sleep seemed impossible. The shaking and rattling of the uncomfortable " gharry," the strange shadows of the trees, and the dark waste of paddy fields stretching before and around us, faintly showing in the mysterious grey light of the dawn, all combined to prevent me from following my brother's example.

On and on we drove along that interminable road, cramped, weary, and impatient; I sat in silence with closed eyes, waiting longingly for the end of our journey, wondering what strange people inhabited this dreary tract of land, and dreaming of the possible adventures to be encountered in the wild country towards which we were travelling.

Suddenly the gharry stopped abruptly ; there was a loud cry from the gharry wallah, a confused medley of Burmese voices, and I sprang up to find we were surrounded by a large body of evil looking men, armed with "dahs." We were "held up" by dacoits !

My brother started up, shouting eager threats and imprecations to the men, and sprang from the carriage. I caught a glimpse of him surrounded by natives, fighting fiercely with his back to the carriage door, while he shouted to me to hand him his revolver from the back seat of the gharry.

But ere I could do so, my attention was called to the matter of my own safety. Three natives had come round to my side of the gharry, the door was wrenched open, and a hugh native flourishing a large "dah" rushed at me, evidently with the intention of procuring the revolver himself.

At that moment all feelings of fear left me, and I only felt furiously angry. Quickly I seized my large roll of bedding, and pulling it down before me received the blow in the folds; then when the knife was buried in the clothes, I crashed the revolver with all my force in the face of the dacoit, and he fell unconscious at my feet, leaving the " dah " in my possession.

The remaining natives rushed at me, and I had no time to lose. Pulling down my brother's bedding roll, I doubled my defence, and from behind it endeavoured to stab at the attacking natives with the captured "dah," dodging their blows behind my barricade. The door of the gharry was narrow, and they could only come at me one at a time.

After playing "bo peep" over my blankets for a little time, they retired, and I was just turning to assist my brother, when suddenly, they rushed my defence, one behind the other, pushed over my barricade with me under it, fell on the top themselves, and we all rolled a confused heap on the bottom of the gharry.

At that moment the man at the pony's head relaxed his hold on the bridle, and the animal, with a speed and energy unusual in Burmese ponies, escaped and galloped down the road, dragging behind it the battered gharry, on the floor of which I and the two natives were struggling.

Faster and faster went the pony, till we seemed to be flying through the air, the door hanging open, and we three fighting for life inside. I made haste to crawl under a seat, and again barricaded myself with my bedding roll, but it was quite clear to me that the struggle could not last much longer ; I was at my wit's end, and my strength was nearly exhausted.

Then the natives climbed on to the seat opposite, and pulled and pushed my barricade, until at last I could hold it no longer. They dragged it away, and threw it from the gharry. My neck was seized between two slimy brown hands, I was pulled from my hiding place, a dark evil looking face peered gloatingly into mine, and then I suppose I lost consciousness, for I remember nothing more until————I awoke, and found we had arrived at the foot of the hills ; not a dacoit had we encountered, and the whole affair had been only a dream.   E

I was disappointed : I feel I shall never be so heroic again, or have such another opportunity for the display of my bravery.

I cannot remember the name of the village at the foot of the hills where we found our ponies waiting, and I certainly could not spell it if I did. It consisted of a mere half a dozen native huts, set down by the road side, and looked a most deserted little place. While our ponies were saddled, and our baggage transferred from the gharry to the bullock cart in attendance, we walked round the village, very glad to stretch our legs after the cramped ride.

All the natives stared at us, as they went leisurely about their daily work ; the girls in their brightly coloured, graceful dresses, going slowly to the well, carrying their empty kerosene oil cans, the almost universal water pots of the Burman ; the men lounging about, smoking big cheroots, and evidently lost in deep meditation ; and the old women sitting in their low bamboo huts, grinding paddy, cooking untempting looking mixtures, or presiding over the sale of various dried fruits and other articles, for in Burmah there is rarely a house where something is not sold.

On the whole, we on our part did not excite very much interest. It needs more than the advent of two strangers to rouse the contemplative Burman from his habitual state of dreaminess.

In one hut I saw a family sitting round their meal, laughing and chatting merrily, while a wee baby, clad in gorgeous silk attire (it looked like the mother's best dress) danced before them in the funniest and most dignified manner, encouraged and coached by an elder sister, aged about seven. They looked such a merry party that I quite longed to join them, for I was beginning to feel hungry, but I changed my mind on a nearer view of the breakfast, a terrible mixture of rice and curried vegetables, with what looked remarkably like decayed fish for a relish.

All this time, though outwardly calm and happy, I was inwardly suffering from ever increasing feelings of dread at the

thought of the ordeal before me.   As I have
explained elsewhere, I have always had a
terror of horses, and had not ridden for
eleven years, not in fact since I was a child,
and then I invariably fell off with or without
any provocation.   But here was I, with
twenty-six miles of rough road between me
and my destination, and no way of
traversing that distance save on horseback.
Knowing my peculiarities, my brother had
begged the very quietest pony from the
police lines at Mandalay, the animal
bearing this reputation stood saddled
before me, and I couldt hink of no further
excuse for longer delaying our start.

Accordingly, I advanced nervously towards the pony, who looked at me out of
the corners of his eyes in an inexplicable
manner, and after three unsuccessful
attempts, and much unwonted embracing
of my brother, I at last succeeded in
mounting, and the reins (an unnecessary
number of them it seemed to me) were
thrust into my hands.

I announced myself quite comfortable
and ready to start ; may Heaven forgive

the untruth ! But evidently my steed was not prepared to depart. I "clucked" and shook the reins, and jumped up and down on the saddle in the most encouraging way, but the pony made no movement.

My brother, already mounted and off, shouted to me to "come on." It was all very well to shout in that airy fashion, I couldn't well "come on" without the pony, and the pony wouldn't.

At last he did begin to move, backwards !

This was a circumstance for which I was wholly unprepared. If a horse runs away, naturally, he is to be stopped by pulling the reins, but if he runs away backwards, there seems nothing to be done; whipping only encourages him to run faster. I tried to turn the pony round, so that if he persisted in continuing to walk backwards, we might at any rate progress in the right direction, but he preferred not to turn, and I did not wish to insist, lest he should become annoyed ; to annoy him at the very outset of the journey I felt would be the height of imprudence.

The natives of the village gathered

round, and with that wonderful capacity for innocent enjoyment for which the Burmese are noted, watched the performance with the deepest interest and delight, while I could do nothing but try to appear at ease, as though I really preferred to travel in that manner.

At last however, my brother would wait no longer, and shouting to the orderly and sais, he made them seize the bridle of my wilful pony, and drag us both forcibly from the village.

And so we started.

Oh! that ride—what a nightmare it was! The pony justified his reputation, and was certainly the most quiet animal imaginable. He preferred not to move at all, but when forced to do so, the pace was such that a snail could easily have given him fifty yards start in a hundred, and a beating, without any particular exertion. He did not walk, he crawled.

In vain did I encourage him in every language I knew, in vain did the sais and orderly ride behind beating him, or in front pulling him, our efforts were of no

avail. Once or twice, under great per-
suasion, he broke into what faintly
suggested a trot, for about two minutes,
but speedily relapsed again into his former
undignified crawl.

My brother at last lost patience and rode
on ahead, leaving me to the tender mercies
of the sais, who, no longer under the eye
of his master, and seeing no reason to
hurry, soon ceased his efforts, and we
jogged on every minute more slowly, till I
fell into a sleepy trance, dreaming that I
should continue thus for ever, riding slowly
along through the silent Burmese jungle,
wrapped in its heavy noon-day sleep, till
I too should sink under the spell of the
sleep god, and become part of the silence
around me.

But the scenery was glorious, and I had
ample time to admire it. Our road wound
up the side of a jungle clad hill, around and
above us rose other hills covered with the
gorgeous vari-coloured jungle trees and
shrubs. Immediately below us lay a deep
wooded ravine, shut in by the hills, and
far away behind us stretched miles and

miles of paddy fields and open country shrouded in a pale blue-grey mist. I cannot imagine grander scenery; what most nearly approach it are views in Saxon Switzerland, but the latter can be compared only as an engraving to a painting, the colour being lacking.

What most impressed me was the absolute silence, and the utter absence of any sign of human life. All round us lay miles and miles of unbroken jungle, inhabited only by birds and beasts; all nature seemed silent, mysterious, and void of human sympathies as in the first days of the world, before man came to conquer, and in conquering to destroy the charm. It is impossible quite to realise this awe-inspiring loneliness of the jungle

"Where things that own not man's dominion dwell."
"And mortal foot hath ne'er or rarely been."

We halted for breakfast at a small way-side village, where we found the usual mat "dâk" bungalow, guarded by the usual extortionate khansamah, and surrounded by the usual dismal compound full of chickens.

Here it was that I made my first acquaintance with the world renowned Burmese chicken, an acquaintance destined to become more and more close, until it blossomed into a deep and never to be forgotten hatred.

The Burmese chicken, whose name is legion, is a thin haggard looking fowl, chiefly noted for his length of leg, and utter absence of superfluous flesh. He picks up a precarious living in the compounds of the houses to which he is attached, and leads a sad, anxious life, owing to the fact that he is generally recognised as the legitimate prey of any man or beast, who at any time of the day or night may be seized with a desire to "chivy."

Consequently he wears a harrassed, expectant look, knowing that the end will overtake him suddenly and without warning. One hour he is happily fighting with his comrades over a handful of grain, within the next he has been killed, cooked, and eaten without pity, though frequently with after feelings of repentance on the part of the eater.

It is, doubtless, the kindly heart of the native cook that prevents him killing the bird more than half an hour before the remains are due at table ; he does not wish to cut off a happy life sooner than is absolutely necessary.   It is, doubtless too, the same gentle heart that induces him to single out for slaughter the most ancient of fowls, leaving the young and tender (if a Burmese chicken ever is tender) still to rejoice in their youth.   If this be so, there is displayed a trait of native character deserving appreciation—which appreciation the result, however, fails as a rule to secure.

It is wonderful what a variety of disguises a Burmese chicken can take upon itself.   The quick change artist is nowhere in comparison.

It appears successively as soup, joint, hash, rissoles, pie, patties and game.   It is covered with rice, onions, and almonds, and raisins, and dubbed ''pillau'' ; it is covered with cayenne pepper and called a savoury.   It is roasted, boiled, baked, potted, and curried, and once I knew an enterprising housekeeper mix it with sardines and serve up a half truth in the shape of "fish cakes."

But under whatever name it may appear, in whatever form it be disguised, it may be invariably recognised by the utter absence of any flavour whatever.

After breakfast, my brother assumed his most stern judicial expression and gave me to understand gently but firmly, that he refused to continue our journey under existing circumstances, and that if I really could not induce my pony to progress faster, I must mount that of the orderly, and leave the laggard to be dealt with by a male hand. I could not object ; I was alone in a distant land far from the protection of my family; I could only agree to the proposal with reluctance, and disclaim all responsibility with regard to my own or the new pony's safety.

Accordingly, the saddles were changed, much to the dissatisfaction of the orderly, and I was speedily mounted on my new steed.

At first the exchange appeared to be an improvement. The pony had a brisk walk, and we progressed quite as rapidly as I wished. I began to feel an accomplished horse-woman, and when my brother suggested a two miles canter, I consented after but a few objections.

We started gaily, and we did canter two miles without a break, and the pony and I did not part company during the proceedings, but that is all I can say.

I have frequently heard foolish people talk of the unspeakable joy of a wild gallop, the delightful motion, the exhilaration of rushing through the air, with a good horse beneath you. Once I listened to such talkers with credulity, now I listen in astonishment. Our gallop was wild enough in all conscience, but after the first three minutes I became convinced it was the most uncomfortable way of getting about I had ever experienced.

I started elegantly enough, gripping my pummel tightly between my knees, and sitting bolt upright, but I soon gave up all ideas of putting on unnecessary "side" of that sort; this ride was no fancy exhibition, it was grim earnest.

I and the pony were utterly out of sympathy with one another, and I am sure the latter did all he could to be tiresome out of pure "cussedness." Whenever I bumped down, he seemed to bump up, and the result was painful; whenever I pulled the reins he merely tossed his head scornfully; and I am sure the saddle must have been slipping about (though it appeared firm enough afterwards), for I landed on all parts of it in turn.

To add to my troubles my sola topee became objectionable.

It was not an ordinary looking topee; it being my first visit to the East, of course I had procured an exceedingly large one, and in addition to its great size, it was very heavy and very ugly. I fancy it was originally intended to be helmet shaped, but its maker had allowed his imagination to run away with him, and when finished, it was the most extraordinary looking headdress that ever spoilt the appearance of a naturally beautiful person.

It resembled rather a swollen plum pudding in a very large dish, than a respectable sola topee.

It was so constructed inside as to fit no existingly shaped human head, and consequently required to be balanced with the greatest care. By dint of sitting very upright I had succeeded in keeping it on my head during the earlier stages of my journey, but now I had more important matters to think of than sola topees, and consequently it became grievously offended, and (being abnormally sensitive, as are most deformed creatures) it commenced to wobble about in a most alarming manner.

On and on we went. I had almost ceased to have any feeling in my legs and body, and began to wonder vaguely what strange person's head had got on to my shoulders, it seemed to fit so loosely. We flew past the second milestone, but my brother, who rode just ahead of me, absorbed no doubt in the joys of the gallop, never stayed his reckless course. I could not stop my pony, because both hands were, of course, engaged in holding on to the saddle. I lost my stirrup; it was never any good to me, but my foot felt lonely without it. My knees were cramped, my head ached, and finally my sola topee, unable longer to endure its undignified wobble, descended slowly over my face and hung there by its elastic, effectually blocking out everything from my sight.

I would have infinitely preferred to have fallen off, but did not know how to do so comfortably.

At last, with a mighty effort I crouched in the saddle, gingerly released one hand, pushed aside the topee from before my mouth, and yelled to my brother to stop. He turned, saw something unusual in my appearance, and, thank goodness! stopped.

It could not have lasted much longer; either I or the pony would have been obliged to give way. When I indignantly explained to my brother what the pony had been doing, all he said was that he hoped to goodness I had not given it a sore back. I know its back could not have been a quarter as sore as was mine! I did not gallop again that or any other day.

We spent the night in another "dâk" bungalow, consisting of three mat walled sleeping apartments, scantily furnished, and an open veranda where we dined. We dined off chicken variously disguised, and being very stiff and weary, retired early to bed.

During dinner, my brother casually remarked that on his last visit there he had killed a snake in the roof, and on retiring to my room I remembered his words and trembled.

I don't know much about snakes, save only that a "king cobra" alone will attack without provocation ; therefore, if one is attacked, the reptile is almost certain to be a snake of that species.

What precautions should therefore be taken to defend one's life I have not ascertained, but I give the information as affording at any rate some satisfaction in case of attack.

The roof of my room was thatched, and looked the very dwelling place of snakes, and how could I possibly defend myself from attack (supposing king cobras inhabited that district), when they might drop down on me while I slept, or come up through the chinks and holes in the wooden floor, and bite my feet when I was getting into bed ? The situation was a desperate one. What was to be done ?

After half an hour, I was forced to abandon my plan of sitting up all night on the table, under my green sun-umbrella ; the table was so rickety that I fell off whenever I dozed, and the situation became painful.

At last a new plan occurred to me. I took a wild leap from the table to the bed, and succeeded in rigging up a tent with the mosquito curtain props, and a sheet. Then, secure from all dangers from below or above, I fell fast asleep, and awoke next morning to find myself still alive and unharmed.

I am convinced that more than one cunning serpent that night returned foiled to its lair, having at last encountered a degree of cunning surpassing its own.

We made an early start next morning, as we had still twelve miles to ride before the day grew hot.

F

The orderly objected to ride further on a snail, and had put my saddle once more on my original pony, so I finished my ride without further mishap.

It was a delicious morning; the early lights and shadows of dawn and sunrise enhanced the beauty of the richly coloured jungle bordering the road. On all sides we were surrounded by the tall, dark, waving trees, and the thick green, pink, golden, and red-brown under-growth, save occasionally when the close bushes were cleared a little, and we caught tempting glimpses of shady moss covered glades, chequered by the sunlight peering through the thick leaves. Everything was very still, and except for the soft whisper of the jungle grass, a great silence brooded over all.

Suddenly there broke upon my ears a strange sound, weird, mystic, wonderful. It was a heavy, grating, creaking noise, more horrible than aught I had heard before. Nearer and nearer it came; and now it could be distinguished as the cry of some mighty beast in pain, for the first and fundamental noise was varied by shrill screams and deep, painful groans. Was it a wounded elephant? No! surely no living elephant ever gave voice to such terrible, awe-inspiring sounds. It must be some far mightier beast, some remnant of the prehistoric ages, which remained still to drag out a lonely existence, hidden from human eyes, in this far Burmese jungle.

But now it was close upon us ; the noise was deafening, making day hideous ; round the corner of the road appeared four huge horns, two meek looking white heads, and ——a bullock cart.

That was the sole cause of this hideous disturbance, of these ear-piercing shrieks which rent the air. As usual, the wheels of the cart were formed of solid circles of wood, not even rounded, and carefully unoiled, and from these emanated those horrible shrieks, groans, and creaks, which are the delight and security of the Burmese driver, and the terror of tigers and panthers haunting the road.

How eminently peaceful must be the life of the bullock-cart driver ! He knows

, no hurry, no anxiety, no responsibility.

Hour after hour, day after day he jogs along, seated on the front of his cart, occasionally rousing himself to joke and gossip with friends he may meet on the way, or to encourage his team by means of his long bamboo stick, but more often he sits wrapped in a deep sleep, or meditation, trusting for guidance to the meek solemn-faced bullocks which he drives. His work is done, his life is passed in one long contin-uous, sleeping, smoking, and eating sort of existence; the thought of such a life of careless, uneventful, unambitious happiness, is appalling.

I grew somewhat weary of the frequent opportunities I had of studying the bul-lock carts and their drivers during that morning ride. Every cart jogged on its noisy way along the very centre of the road; but it is not meet that a Sahib and a representative of the great Queen should occupy anything but the very centre of the road when taking his rides abroad. Con-sequently whenever we met a bullock cart both cavalcades had to stop. It was a

BURMESE BULLOCK CART

work of time to make the driver hear the orderly's voice, above the creaking of the wheels; more time was occupied in rousing him from his sleep, and explaining to him the situation ; and more time again in explaining matters to the bullocks, and inducing them to drag the cart into the ditch.

It took five minutes to pass each cart, and as we met a great many that morning as we approached the village, our progress was considerably delayed. I should have preferred for the sake of speed to have ridden in the ditch myself; at the same time I am aware such opinions are unworthy of the relation of an Indian Civilian.

My entrance into Remyo, the future scene of my experiences, at half-past ten that morning was striking, though hardly dignified.

Picture to yourself a sorrowful, huddled figure, seated on a weary dishevelled looking pony, covered from head to foot with red dust, and surmounted by a large battered topee " tip-tilted like the petal of a flower." I had long ceased to make any pretence at riding. I sat sideways on my saddle, as one sits in an Irish car, grasping in one hand the pummel and in the other my large green sun umbrella, for the sun was terribly hot. How weary I was, and how overjoyed at arriving at my destination !

But even yet my troubles were not over. There was the house, there my sister waiting in the veranda to welcome me, but directly my pony arrived at the gate of the compound he stopped dead. Apparently it was not in the bond that I should be carried up to the door, and so no further would he go. I was too impatient to argue the matter, too weary to give an exhibition of horsemanship, so there was nothing to do but descend, walk up the compound, and tumble undignifiedly into the house, where the first thing I did was to register a vow that never again, except in a case of life and death, would I attempt to ride a Burmese pony.

CHAPTER V.

AN UP-COUNTRY STATION.

"Far from the madding crowd's ignoble strife."—(Gray.)

I DARESAY that Remyo is very like other small up-country stations in Burmah, but to me it appeared to be the very end of the earth, so different was it from all I had expected. It stands in a small valley, surrounded by low jungle-clad hills. The clearing is perhaps three miles long by one and-a-half wide, but there always appeared to be more jungle than clearing about the place, so quickly does the former spread.

The Station is traversed crosswise by two rough tracks called by courtesy roads, and is surrounded by what is imposingly termed "The Circular Road." This road, but recently constructed, is six or seven miles long, and passes mostly outside the clearing, being consequently bordered in many places on both sides by thick jungle.

There is something infinitely pathetic to my mind about this poor new road, wandering aimlessly in the jungle, leading nowhere and used by no one. At regular distances there stand by the wayside tall posts bearing numbers. The lonely posts mark the situations of houses which it is hoped will, in the future, be built on the allotments which they represent. In theory, the circular road is lined with houses, for Remyo has a great future before it ; but just at present, the future is travelling faster than the station, and consequently the poor road is allowed to run sadly into the jungle alone, its course known only to the dismal representatives of these future houses.

The only finished building near which this road passes is the railway station, a neat wooden erection, possessing all the requirements of a small wayside station, and lacking only one essential feature—a railway, for the railway, like the great future of Remyo, is late in arriving, and so the road and the railway station are left sitting sadly expectant in the jungle, waiting patiently for the arrival of that future which alone is needed to render them famous.

In Remyo itself there is a fair sized native bazaar, consisting of rows of unpleasant looking mat huts, each raised a few feet from the ground, with sloping overhanging roofs, and open sides. The road through the bazaar is always very dusty, crowded with bullock carts, goats, and dogs, and usually alive with naked Burmese babies of every age and size. Not a pleasant resort on a hot day.

Besides the bazaar, the station contains the Court House, the District Bungalow, and the Post Office; half-a-dozen European houses scattered up and down the clearing, and the club.

To the Anglo-Indians the club seems as necessary to existence as the air they breathe. I verily believe that when the white man penetrates into the interior to found a colony, his first act is to clear a space and build a club house.

The Club House at Remyo is a truly imposing looking edifice, perched high on

the hill side, standing in a well kept compound, surrounded by its offices, bungalows,
and stables. About the interior of the building I must confess ignorance, it being an
unpardonable offence for any woman to
cross the threshold. It may be that it is
but a whited sepulchre, the exterior
beautiful beyond description, the interior
merely emptiness : I cannot tell.

At the foot of the Club House stands a
tiny, one-roomed, mat hut, the mostun pre-
tentious building I ever beheld, universally
known by the imposing title of "The
Ladies Club." Here two or more ladies of
the station nightly assemble for an hour
before dinner, to read the two months old
magazines, to search vainly through the
shelves of the "library" for a book they
have not read more than three times, to
discuss the iniquities of the native cook,
and to pass votes of censure on the male
sex for condemning them to such an
insignificant building.

It has always been a sore point with the
ladies of Remyo that their Club House
only contains one room. They argue that

if half the members wish to play whist, and the other half wished to talk, many inconveniences (to say the least) would arise. As there are but four lady members of the club, this argument does not appear to me to be convincing, but I do not pretend to understand the intricacies of club life.

I have sometimes been tempted to believe that the ladies would really be happier without a club; possessing one, they feel strongly the necessity of using it, and though they would doubtless prefer sometimes to sit comfortably at home, every evening sees them sally forth determinedly to their tiny hut. There they sit night after night till nearly dark, and then, not daring to disturb the lordly occupants of the big house, to demand protection, they steal home nervously along the jungle bordered road, trembling at every sound, but all the time talking and laughing cheerfully, in order to convince everybody (themselves in particular) that they are not at all afraid of meeting a panther or tiger, in fact would rather prefer to do so than not. Truly the precious club is not an unmixed blessing !

There are a few wooden houses in Remyo, but the majority are merely built of matting, with over-hanging roofs. They are often raised some twenty feet above the ground, and present the extraordinary appearance of having grown out of their clothes like school boys.

The house in which my sister and her husband lived was a wooden erection of unpretentious appearance. I cannot say who was the architect, but a careful consideration of the construction of the house revealed to us much of his method.

In the first place he was evidently an advocate of the benefits of fresh air and light. The house was all doors and windows, not one of them, apparently, intended to shut, and not satisfied with this, the builder had carefully left wide chinks in the walls, and two or three large holes in the roof. The front door opened directly into the drawing-room, the drawing-room into the dining room, the dining-room into the bedrooms, and the bedrooms on to the compound again. Thus we were enabled in all weathers to have a direct draught through the house, and as Remyo is a remarkably windy place, much of our time was occupied in preventing the furniture from being blown away. Whenever anything was missing we invariably found it in the back compound, whither it had been carried by the wind. Life in such an atmosphere was no doubt healthy, but a trifle wearing to the nerves.

The compactness of the house was delightful. All the rooms led out of one another, and there were no inside doors, consequently one could easily carry on a conversation with those in other parts of the house without leaving one's chair or raising one's voice.

The only occasion on which we found this arrangement of the rooms inconvenient was when we stained the dining room floor. The stain did not dry for three days, and during that time all communication between the drawing room and bedrooms was entirely cut off, for the only way from one to the other was through the dining room, and that was impossible, unless we wished our beautiful floor to be covered with permanent foot marks.

Our architect was evidently a dweller in the plains, and the uses of a fireplace were unknown to him. In each of the small bedrooms he had built large open fireplaces, worthy of a baronial hall, while in neither of the sitting rooms was there the slightest vestige of a fireplace of any sort or kind whatever.

This was a little inconvenient. Naturally an affectionate and gregarious family party, we did not like to spend our evenings, each sitting alone before our own palatial bedroom fireplace ; being properly brought up, and proud of our drawing room, we preferred to occupy it, and often, as I sat shivering while the wind tore through the rooms, whistling and shrieking round the furniture, and the rain poured through the roof, I wondered what was supposed to be the use of a house at all ; we should have done quite as well without one, except, of course, for the look of the thing.

Modern inventions such as bells appear unknown in Remyo. If you want anything you must shout for it until you get it.

When calling on a neighbour you stand outside the front door, and shout for five minutes, if no one appears in that time, you assume they are not at home, put your cards on the doorstep or through a chink in the wall, and depart. It is a primitive arrangement, but still, not without advantages. If you don't wish to find people at home, you shout softly.

We were superior to all our neighbours in the possession of a bell. We hung it up in the compound near the servants' "go downs," and passed the bell rope through various holes in the walls, etc., to the dining room. I don't know where the bell originally came from, but I think it must have come from a pagoda, for it was undoubtedly bewitched. It rang at all hours of the day and night without provocation. Once it pealed out suddenly at midnight and rang steadily for half-an-hour, when it as suddenly stopped. This was probably caused by some birds swinging on the rope, but it was most uncanny.

The servants used to answer the bell at first when it rang in the day time, until the joke palled on them, and they became suddenly deaf to its call. They never answered it at night : I fancy they thought when they heard it then, that the house was attacked by dacoits or tigers and we were ringing for help, and they deemed it more prudent to remain shut up in their " go downs." When we attempted to ring the bell with a purpose, it invariably stuck somewhere and would not sound. We never ceased to feel proud of the possession of our bell, but ceased at last to expect it to be of any practical use.

When my sister first showed me over her house, my heart sank in spite of my ostensible admiration, for where was the kitchen ? Did dwellers in Remyo eat no cooked food ; must I be satisfied with rice and fruits ? However, my doubts were soon set at rest when we visited the compound, for there stood a tiny tin shed,

inside which was a broad brick wall, with
three holes for fires, and what looked like
a dog kennel, but which I learned was the
oven. A fire was lighted inside the oven,
and when the walls were red hot the burning logs were pulled out, the bread placed
in, and walled up.

How anyone managed to cook anything
successfully thus was a marvel to me. I
had gone out to Remyo, fresh from a course
of scientific cooking lectures, intending to
rejoice the palates of the poor exiles with
the dainty dishes I would cook for their
edification. When I saw that kitchen,
and when I learned that such a thing as a
pair of scales did not exist in the station,
all measuring being done by guess work, I
gave up all hope of fulfilling my intention,
and looked upon the native cook as
the most talented gentleman of my
acquaintance.

The furniture in Remyo is of the "let-
us-pack-up-quickly-and-remove" type. It
is of the lightest and most unsubstantial
kind, and has the air of having seen many
sales and many owners.

G

The most prominent article in nearly every house is the deck chair, faithful and much travelled chair, which has accompanied its master over the sea from England, and wandered with him into many a dreary little out-of-the-way village, where perchance he sees for months no fellow white man, and where his chair and pipe alone receive his confidences, and solace his soul in the utter loneliness of the jungle. No wonder then that the deck chair wears an important air, and regards other pieces of furniture, which probably change owners every six months, with contemptuous scorn.

The impossibility of having a settled home in Burmah is very pathetic. In Rangoon, the interior of the houses occasionally wear a settled and homelike appearance, but in the jungle, never. Everything is selected with a view to quick packing ; pictures, ornaments, and useless decorations are reduced to a minimum, and only articles of furniture which are indispensable are seen. When one is liable to be moved elsewhere at four days' notice, there is no encouragement to take deep root, the frequent uprooting would be too painful.

This spirit of constant change seems to enter into the blood of the Anglo-Indian, for the housewife is perpetually moving her furniture, "turning her rooms round" so to speak, and she never seems to keep anything in the same place for more than a week !

After all, not Burmah, but England is looked upon as "Home." Even the man of twenty-five years service whose family, friends, and interests may be all centred in Burmah, who loves the life he leads there, and is proud of the position he holds, even he talks of what he will do when he " goes home," and in imagination crowns with a halo "this little precious stone set in the silver sea, this blessed plot, this earth, this realm, this England," which no amount of fog, cold, monotony, and dreary oblivion in his after life here, ever dispels. However happy and prosperous the Anglo-Indian may be in his exile, going to England, is " going home."

Our most unique piece of furniture was the piano.

I do not remember who was the maker of this renowned instrument, but its delicate constitution was most unhappily disorganised by the climate. When first it came to us it was quite a nice piano, rather jingling, and not always in tune, but "fit to pass in a crowd with a shove." Alas! the Remyo climate was fatal; the degeneration commenced at once, and proceeded so rapidly, that in three months all was over.

The first indication of trouble was a serious feud between several of the notes, which would persist in making use of one another's tones, and would not work in harmony. For example, when one struck C sharp, it promptly sang out high F's tone, and high F, being deprived of its lawful voice, was forced to adopt a sound like nothing we had ever heard before. Then E flat became officious and conceited, and persisted in sounding its shrill note through the whole of the piece in performance, while G on the contrary was sulky, and wouldn't sound at all.

Now all this was, of course, most disconcerting to other notes which had hitherto
behaved in an exemplary manner. Some
became flurried and nervous, and sang
totally wrong tones, or sounded their own
in such a doubtful, apologetic manner that
it was of very little effect. Others grew
annoyed, sided with various leaders in the
quarrels, jangling together noisily, and
persisting in sounding discords and inter-
rupting each other. Others again were
seized with a mischievous spirit ; they
mocked and mimicked their companions,
and vied with one another in producing
the most extraordinary and unpleasant
noises.

Chaos and anarchy reigned in the piano
case, all laws of sound and harmony were
o'erthrown, the bass clef could no longer
be trusted to produce a low note, nor the
treble a high one, and a chromatic scale
produced such an extraordinary conglom-
eration of sounds, as would certainly have
caused a German band to die of envy.

This could not continue for ever, and at
last came reaction. Whether caused by

the quarterly visit of the Mandalay chaplain, or by the shocked and pained expression on the face of a musical friend who called one day when I was sounding (it could no longer be called playing) the piano, I know not, but certain it is, the piano was suddenly seized with remorse. Notes conquered their thieving propensities, differences were patched up, discord and jangling ceased, and the whole community, as a sign of real repentance, took upon itself the vow of silence.

Not a sound could we extract from the once noisy keys, save occasionally a sad whisper from the treble, or a low murmur from the bass. After a time, even these ceased, and the once harmonious and soul-stirring tones of the piano, passed entirely into the Land of Silence.

CHAPTER VI

THE EUROPEAN INHABITANTS.

" In spite of all temptations
To belong to other nations
He remains an Englishman"—
" H.M.S. Pinafore."

THE European population of Remyo is small, consisting in fact of but four resident ladies, and some dozen resident males ; but despite their limited number they form a very friendly and independent little community. Among them are to be found the usual types of Anglo Indian society, but they display characteristics not met with among the dwellers in larger stations.

Remyo is so entirely cut off from civilisation, that the inhabitants must of necessity depend solely upon themselves for amusement, and as entertainments, at which one would invariably meet the same half-dozen guests are apt to become a trifle monotonous, the ladies, deprived of

this usual mode of killing time, are compelled to devote themselves to domestic
pursuits rather more than is the custom
of most Anglo Indians.

The comparative coolness of the climate
(Remyo being 3,500 feet above sea level)
is conducive to such occupations, and
whereas in Rangoon, or Mandalay, housekeeping duties are reduced to a minimum,
in Remyo, the ladies, having nothing else
to do, engage themselves thus with a zeal
and energy worthy of a Dutch housewife.

But, poor souls, they are terribly
handicapped !

In the first place, they are mostly unaccustomed to housekeeping themselves ;
secondly, the servants and household are
quite unaccustomed to being "kept" ; and
thirdly, it is practically impossible for a
mistress to do her own marketing unless
she possess an unusual knowledge of the
language.

She may resolutely keep accounts, lock
up stores, walk about all morning in an
apron, with a large bunch of keys, and
have long confidential conversations with

the cook ; but in spite of all these possibilities she can only play at housekeeping ; the Cook and Head Boy are the real managers of the establishment, and they regard the well meant efforts of their mistress with the kindly amusement one would extend to a child "keeping house." A Remyo lady's morning interview with her cook, usually a Madrassee, is an amusing interlude.

Neither fish nor joints can be procured in the native bazaar, so the poor housekeeper is often at her wits' end to introduce variety into her evening menu.

She begins cheerfully : "Well cook, what have we for dinner to-night ? "

Cook replies laconically, "Chicken."

"Chicken," repeats the mistress doubtfully, "yes, perhaps that will do. Did you kill it yesterday ? "

"No ! missis, not killed yet."

" Oh cook ! " in a tone of stern reproach, "missis told you always to kill it the day before, why have you not done so ? "

Cook shelters himself hehind an unintelligible answer in a mixture of Hindustani and "Pigeon English," and after an unsuccessful attempt to understand him, his mistress is forced to pass from the subject, with a rebuke which he receives with a reproachful look. "Now," she continues, "what have you for soup?"

"Chicken" is again the prompt reply.

"Is there really nothing else?" demands the mistress uneasily.

"No, there is nothing else."

"Well," hopefully, "you must make a very nice little side dish (entrée), what can we have?"

"Nice bit of grilled chicken," suggests cook cheerfully.

"Oh no cook," she cries in despair, "we can't have more chicken."

"What would missis like then?"

Missis has not the vaguest idea of any possible suggestion, so diffidently agrees that perhaps chicken will be nice. She asks about the savoury, but seeing the word "chicken" again hovering on cook's lips, decides to make the savoury herself, and turns to receive the daily accounts.

Then cook rattles off a long account of his expenditure, which his mistress duly enters in her book, fondly hoping that he isn't charging her more than double the cost of each article, but having no means of discovering the truth.

Once or twice, on visits to the bazaar, we asked the price of various things, and triumphantly confronted the cook with the result of our researches, but he was never in the least disconcerted, and at once entered into a long, unintelligible, and quite irrefutable explanation as to why the article was cheaper on that particular day than on any other. It is quite impossible to upset the cheerful sang froid of a Madrassee.

Native servants have the reputation of being most faithful to their master, and perhaps they deserve the character, for they allow no one else to cheat him (unless they get the lion's share of the spoil), but they consider it their special prerogative to cheat him themselves at every opportunity.

A scolding from a mistress makes little

impression on a Madrassee servant,—he receives it with an air of gentle reproach, while he most persistently denies the offence, whatever it may be, from a bad dinner, to a broken plate or an undelivered message. It is only the master, who, by a wealth of strong language, and judiciously directed remarks, concerning the origin, parents, and relations of the guilty one, can hope to make the slightest impression upon the impervious native mind.

A further difficulty for the young and ardent housekeeper is the number of servants in her establishment. One man is engaged to sweep the floor, another to dust the furniture, one to fetch the water, a second to pour it into the bath, one to lay the knives and forks, and a companion to hand the plates, and so on through every department of the household work.

This divided duty is exceedingly convenient to the servants, for if anything be wrong the fault can always be laid on the absent one, or a scolding delivered to one can be passed on almost unlimitedly until everyone has enjoyed an opportunity of relieving his feelings. But it is inconvenient for a mistress ; such a delay is caused in carrying out an order. For example, if a jug of water be spilled, a first servant picks up the jug, a second dries the table cloth, a third dries the table, a fourth mops up the water from the floor, a fifth rearranges the furniture, a sixth carries out the empty jug, and a seventh fetches the water to refill it.

All orders are delivered to the Head Boy, a most important and dignified personage, and he transmits them through the various ranks of his underlings until they reach the servant whose duty it is to carry them out. During the transmission through so many channels, of course the orders become hopelessly mixed.

We had only fourteen servants, as our house was not large ! A few of them, such as the cook, sais, and butler had definite duties, the remainder seemed to be chiefly engaged in getting in one another's way and quarrelling. But I suppose the work of the house could not have been carried on without them, though their number was distinctly inconvenient.

In Rangoon, where servants abound, it would be easy to dismiss and engage a dozen a day, but not so in the remoter stations. The natives of India will not leave the plains unless a strong inducement be offered, and the Burmese much prefer not to work, if they can live without doing so. Burmans are usually excellent servants, but they are slow to learn to speak English, and the young housekeeper, who has probably been accustomed to English, or at least Hindustani-speaking servants in Rangoon, experiences great difficulty in making herself understood.

All our servants, with the exception of the cook, were Burmese, and when my brother happened to be away, and the cook was not at hand to interpret, we felt particularly helpless. Messages brought at such a time had to go undelivered, and many a struggle have I had to understand Po Sin's wants, or to make him understand mine. Housekeeping under such disadvantages is not a happy undertaking.

Another way of passing time in which we indulged, was cooking. It was cooking under difficulties, for the most important part (the baking) had perforce to be entrusted to the tender mercies of the cook, no one else being capable of understanding his intricate oven. And the cook, jealous of our trespass on his prerogative, almost invariably served up our cakes in the guise, either of soft dough, or of black cinders.

The chief objects of our cooking experiments were cakes and savouries. We neither of us knew very much about cooking, but we had cookery books, and did what we could, supplying the place of the innumerable ingredients we did not possess, with any we happened to have on hand. The result was usually distasteful.

I made cakes with exceeding great vigour and confidence during almost the whole of my stay, but nobody ate them save myself from bravado, the dogs from greed, and unsuspecting strangers from innocence.

Cake making was a fashionable subject

of conversation at the ladies' "five o'clocks" in Remyo, and everyone gave everyone else recipes. I was astonished to hear my sister (whom I knew to be almost entirely ignorant upon such subjects) glibly confiding recipes for all sorts of things, on one of these occasions. I taxed her with the matter later, but she explained that it was the fashion to give recipes, and so long as she was careful to include an ingredient or two, impossible to obtain, she could safely trust that no one would find her out.

There is one shop in Remyo in addition to the native Bazaar, and the ladies usually pay it a daily visit, in order, I suppose, to add realism to their pretence of housekeeping.

The method adopted on these occasions is remarkable. No one expects to find anything she really wants in the shop, as it is kept by a native of India, but she begins hopefully asking for various articles, each demand being greeted by a shake of the head. She then asks the shopkeeper what he does happen to sell, at which he appears doubtful, but suggests some useless thing such as antimacassars. The purchaser at length makes a tour of the shop, picks out the least useless article she can find, and bears it home in triumph.

The unwise thing to do, is to order an article from Rangoon or Mandalay. One is indeed lucky if it arrives within twelve months after being ordered, and without an expenditure of all one's powers of sarcasm in letters of remonstrance, and a fortune in stamps.

Firstly, there will be received about a dozen letters, with intervals of four days or so between each, demanding fresh descriptions and explanations of the desired article. Then, when more specific description is an impossibility, letters for money will arrive ; a request for a rupee for carriage, another request for five annas for something else, for half a rupee that has been overlooked in the first account, and so on for four weeks more. Then the article is announced to be upon the way, but it does not arrive. More letters bring to light the fact that it is lost ; has most

H

mysteriously disappeared ; cannot be traced anywhere.

New people come upon the scene. Letters from carriers and agents arrive. Weeks elapse, still the article cannot be found. Another is in course of construction, when it is suddenly discovered that by some strange oversight the original was overlooked, never sent off at all, and is still reposing in the same tiresome shop. At length the once desired purchase arrives, but the purchaser has now long ceased to feel any interest in it whatever.

The inhabitants of Remyo live together in apparent peace and friendliness, but there is between them one never ending source of rivalry, *i.e.* their gardens.

Gardening is one of the most fashionable employments in Remyo. Everyone has a garden, though the uninitiated would probably not recognise the fact, and the amount of time, thought, and energy expended thereon is worthy of better results than those I beheld.

For the " Remyoans" are ambitious folk, and are not content with the flowers, plants and natural products of the country. Their desire is to have a real English garden, and with this end in view, they sow innumerable seeds, set many bulbs, rake, dig and water (or superintend these operations) till life is a burden both to themselves and to their servants.   Possibly, I did not remain long enough, but the results I saw were not satisfactory ; it required a great stretch of imagination to mark any resemblance between a large bare compound covered with coarse jungle grass, dotted about with flat grey-soiled beds containing a few withered looking plants (half-a-dozen violets perhaps, and a haggard sunflower), and an English garden.   Perhaps long absence from home had dulled their recollection of gardens in England.

We were specially unlucky in our garden.   Had we been content to confine our efforts to plants in pots and boxes (as did some of our wiser neighbours) we might have been fairly successful.   But visions of rose gardens, artistically laid out beds, and mossy violet covered dells dazzled us, and our ambitions in this direction were boundless.

The coarse grass, the poor soil, and the persistent reappearances of unsightly jungle weeds in all sorts of unexpected places should have daunted us, but we had souls above such trifles.   Directly we had formed our plans we set to work, scorning the advice of more experienced people, and disregarding all considerations of prepared beds, manure, and seasons.   We marked out several intricately shaped beds, dug them up, lightly scattered some good soil over the top, and proceeded to sow our seed with hearty good will.

The first difficulty we met with was with regard to arrangement.   Each of us had a favourite plan, the abandonment of which no arguments on the part of the others could persuade.   At length, after much useless discussion, we decided each to go our own way, sow our seed where we chose, and leave it to Nature to settle the difficulty.   This was so far satisfactory, tho' we felt anxious when we found that nasturtiums had been sown on the top of daffodil bulbs, and one poor little bed of pansies had a border of sweet peas and sunflowers.

For some days after we had laid out the garden, my sister and I had a wearing time. The first thing in the early mornings we hurried out for an eager search after signs of life in our seeds. We divided the day into watches, that someone might always be at hand to defend the precious seed from the marauding crows and pigeons. The cool of the evening, usually given up to tennis and other amusements, was devoted wholly to the fatiguing task of watering.

At last, sooner in fact than we really expected, we were rewarded by a few delicate green shoots, peering cautiously above the ground. How tenderly we cherished these first fruits of our toil ; how carefully we shaded them from the sun, watered them, and protected them from the evil onslaught of the pigeons. How angry we were when we discovered they were weeds.

However, we were rewarded at last by the unmistakable appearance of cultivated plants. Nearly every seed sent up its little green shoot, and for a few days we

were most unpleasantly proud, and treated
our friends with contemptuous pity, while
we visited and measured the plants almost
every half-hour, to see if they had grown
in the interval.   But our joy was short
lived, for from some cause or another,
either the strong sun, the lack of water,
or the poor soil, all our plants withered
before they put forth flowers.

At first we refused to believe our ill fortune ; we told one another that it was
always thus at first with delicate plants,
that they must have more water and less
sun.   We covered them over in the heat
of the day with waste paper baskets,
topees, and cunningly erected tents of
straw, and we risked our lives a hundred
times, by running out in the hot sun to
replace these, when the wind blew them
away.   We talked bravely of being able
soon to gather bunches of daffodils, and
to send our neighbours baskets of sweet
peas.   But we each felt all the time in our
heart of hearts, that our hopes were
doomed to disappointment.

At last we could keep up the delusion no

longer, and owned the fact of our failure to one another ; and being now sadder and wiser folk, threw away the withered plants, and made a new garden, following this time the advice of our neighbours.

The only plants which did prosper in this first garden were the nasturtiums (I verily believe they will flourish anywhere) and for several hours a tiny bed round the foot of a tree at the bottom of the compound veritably blazed with the colour afforded by four flourishing nasturtiums ; but while we were at the Club that evening, the crows pecked off all the petals of the flowers, and our only success was but a short lived one.

The kitchen garden, which we consigned to the care of Po Sin, our head boy, was rather more successful, our radishes, and mustard and cress being the wonder of the country side.

Then we had good hopes for the peas too ; there was one row about ten inches high which looked really promising, and as we sat on the veranda in the evenings contemplating this cheerful sight, we talked longingly of the time when we should have a dish of our own peas for dinner.

But alas for the vanity of human expectations. One morning, my sister had sallied forth to inspect the garden, when I was startled by the despairing cry of "Come, come at once, the peas are flowering ;" and upon hurrying to the spot I found it too true ; our precocious peas were already in flower, and nothing could be done to discourage them. After a few days the petals fell away, and miniature pea pods, containing microscopic peas appeared in their place. Our wishes were fulfiled ; we had a dish, (a very small one) of our own peas for dinner, but alas it consisted of the produce of the entire row.

Another source of much interest was our strawberry plant. I took 100 strawberry runners out with me from England, but, unfortunately, only one survived, which put forth three new shoots, and appeared for a time quite healthy, but never bore fruit. Still, it may yet do so ; and in the meantime it is much admired by all the inhabitants of Remyo.

Our second garden, happily, being prepared with more regard to the demands of
the climate, was a success, and wiped out
the stain of our first failure.

It is well that the Remyo ladies can
interest themselves in the manner I have
indicated, for between breakfast and tea
time the sun is so terribly hot, as to render
out-door exercise quite impossible, and in
the absence of many books time is sometimes difficult to kill.

Ladies in England, with their hundred
and one occupations, their amusements,
household duties, and perhaps charities to
attend to, can have but a very faint conception of how wearisomely long and
lonely are some days, to their Anglo-
Indian sisters. Their husbands away, or
busy much of the day, deprived of their
children's society, with few books, few
amusements, and practically no duties, life
is far from being an unqualified joy to
these exiled women. Let the British
matron who would accuse her Eastern
sister of idleness, frivolity, and worse, consider these things, and forbear to judge.

The men, with their work and sport to engage their time, are less apt to find the days long ; but even they at times feel the same strain. Indeed, I remember one day, when there was no work to be done, my brother and sister, (who had but lately left Rangoon with its constant whirl of gaiety) became so hopelessly and desperately bored, that we were reduced to revive our drooping spirits by making sugar toffee over the spirit kettle.

Before breakfast and after tea are the opportunities for exercise and amusement, and the most is made of these cooler hours.

Remyo boasts a gravel tennis court, and a nine-hole golf course, mostly bunkers. Two more tennis courts, and a cricket and polo ground are in course of construction, preparatory to the arrival of the Great Future to which I have referred. Each form of exercise enjoys about three days popularity at a time. At one time tennis will be the rage, and every one repairs to the Club court, tho' so short are the evenings before sunset, that it is impossible to play more than three sets an afternoon, so we are forced to be content with about three games each.   Then the tennis rage dies away, and golf suddenly becomes the fashionable game.

Like most occupations in Remyo, golf is golf under difficulties, though personally, whenever and wherever I play golf, I play under difficulties.   The links are chiefly jungle, and a wood axe would probably be the most useful accessory to the enjoyment of the game.   The holes are short, and a good player would probably drive on to the green every time, but at Remyo we were not good players.   If by some lucky chance one drove perfectly straight, there was nothing worse to fear than a tree, or a deep nullah, filled with reeds and hoof marks, a nullah where might be spent a harassing quarter of an hour, slashing at a half hidden ball, which, in sheer desperation, one was at last compelled to pick out.   But if the drive were not straight, then what endless and interesting possibilities or impossibilities were revealed. Heaps of stones, inpenetrable bushes, reeds, rabbit-holes, and every form of acute misery which the golfer's soul can conceive.

Yet the Links are very popular, and are the scene of many an exciting match, in spite of lost balls, broken clubs, and lost tempers. I have seen three clubs broken by one man in an afternoon's match, and he was neither a particularly bad player, nor especially violent.

The Burman is not a success as a caddie. Our loogalays looked upon the game at first with indifference, then with dislike. I think they imagined that we purposely drove the ball into a hopeless tangle of grass and bushes in order to scold them when they could not find it. They could never be induced to make any distinction between the clubs, and looked hurt when we curtly refused to drive with our putters. Their notion of marking balls, too, is very primitive ; Po Mya only found one during my stay, which it turned out was an old one lost some days before. In fine, they seemed to think it the greatest folly that we should tramp up and down, and in and out of nullahs, and lose our tempers

so unnecessarily, because of a small white
ball, when we had plenty more at home.

On some afternoons everyone will repair
to the new polo and cricket ground, and
walk up and down the new laid turf, discussing solemnly the drainage, and general
advantages and disadvantages of the
position ; or, feeling energetic, will practise
cricket, and the knowing ones will give
exhibitions of tricky polo strokes.

The making of the polo ground was
seriously delayed at first on account of the
divergent opinions as to the best site, each
declaring his selection to be the only one
possible, and showering unlimited contempt
upon all others.   Every day we were
dragged off to inspect a new spot, and all
appeared to me so equally lacking in points
of advantage, that I had no difficulty in
impressing each new discoverer with my
knowledge in such matters, by disparaging
(in confidence) all other schemes than his.

Finally, a site was chosen, and while the
ground was in course of construction, those
whose views had been disregarded, derived
the satisfaction (always to be had in such

cases) of discussing the insurmountable obstacles to the selected proposal.

Some afternoons were devoted to rides. The jungle around Remyo is lovely, tho' not being there during the Rains, I did not see it to perfection. There are delightful rides in every direction, and exquisite views from the hills, whence can be seen for miles nothing but undulating waves of jungle, every colour from deepest reds and browns to the bright pink of the peach blossom, and the pale green of the feathery bamboos. It is a wonderful sight, this unbroken jungle, bordered in the far distance by the shadowy blue hills of the Shan States.

Sometimes we visited quaint pagodas, with their neighbouring pretty, many-roofed kyaungs where the yellow robed hpoongyis, wander in meditation, or study 'neath the shade of the palm and banana groves. The pagodas are all very similar in shape, and near to each is a tazoung full of images of Gaudama, with ever the. same calm peaceful smile, denoting a philosophy superior to the cares and artificialities of the world around.

Sometimes we rode along narrow jungle paths, bordered by a tangled mass of bright coloured bushes and undergrowth, or by the tall, waving, jungle grass, which is always whispering. These paths lead to tiny collections of bamboo huts, surrounded by high fences to keep out dacoits and other marauders, where the unambitious native leads a peaceful, contented life, under the shadow of the bamboos and peepul trees ; an uneventful existence, enlivened, perhaps, occasionally by a Pwé, or visit to a pagoda feast at a neighbouring village.

I enjoyed these expeditions, tho' they were ever fraught with danger to my limbs. Nothing would induce me again to mount a pony (I had had sufficient experience) so I accompanied the others on my bicycle.

Of late years many wonderful bicycle riders have exhibited their tricks to the public, but I am certain none have performed such extraordinary feats as are called for by the state of the Burmese roads, most of them mere jungle tracks, ploughed in every direction into deep ruts by the

bullock carts.   It was impossible to ride
in the furrows, as they were not sufficiently
wide to allow the pedals to work round, so
I was obliged to perform a sort of plank
riding trick along the top of the rut.
Occasionally, my eminence would break off
abruptly, and unless the bicycle succeeded
in jumping the gap a fall was inevitable.
Never had bicycle such severe usage,
nor ever did such yeoman service as
mine; but save an occasional twist
of the handle bars, or a bent spoke, I
never met with a serious accident, and I
soon learned the art of "falling softly."

My anxieties, too, were increased by the
mistaken kindness of my companions, who
would persist in riding beside me and
conversing.   One man in particular (I
have forgiven him, for I know he meant
it kindly) would never consent to leave me
to ride alone.   He would trot along on his
pony, either just beside, or worse still just
behind me, when I felt I might fall at any
moment, and that he could not help riding
over me.   He would chatter away gaily,
while I, with agonised expression,

struggled along, one eye on the road and one eye on the pony, scarce heeding his remarks, making the most hopelessly vague replies to his questions, and commiting myself to I know not what opinions.

One day we actually took a walk. We ladies grew weary of our customary amusements, and though we had none of us done much walking since we left England, we hailed the new idea with delight. The men refused to accompany us (the English civilian in the East seems to forget how to walk) so we went with only a servant or two to carry our cameras, refreshments, and other necessities.

We walked about five miles thro' the jungle, to a little native village surrounded entirely by clumps of feathery bamboos, a most exquisite spot. We climbed a neighbouring hill where stood the inevitable pagoda and kyaung, and were rewarded by a perfect view.

Our photographic intentions were unfulfilled, for as we were about to focus our cameras, a jungle fire was set alight below, and the smoke, drifting across the

I

valley towards us most effectually obscured our view.   We were forced to be content with photographing one another, the most beautiful substitutes we could find.

We examined the pagoda, peeped into the kyaung, and tried to induce the hpoongyi to come out and be photographed ; but the pious man, evidently a hermit, shut himself promptly into the inner recesses of his dwelling, and continued to read in a loud voice until we had taken our departure.   We thought him un-necessarily suspicious, and should have been hurt had we not felt it to be really rather a compliment to our charms.

Our expedition was on the whole a success, but as we arrived home very hot and tired, having lost our way once or twice, we failed to convince the stay-at-homes that we had enjoyed ourselves without them.

One morning early, my sister and I were startled by a succession of shots which rang out close to the house.   My brother was away in the district, making an official tour among the villages under his charge, so we were alone and unprotected. Hurrying to the window, what was our astonishment to see a band of Goorkhas, under command of one of the subalterns, of the detachment stationed at Remyo, defending our house against an unseen enemy who lurked in the neighbouring jungle, and kept up an incessant firing. My mind first flew to dacoits, then to French or Chinese (I knew there had been trouble on the border), then, on catching sight of one of the enemy, and recognising him also as a Goorkha, I knew mutiny must have broken out. Trouble of this kind always breaks out unexpectedly, I have heard.

Soon however, we were forced to suppose that it must be a revolution, for leading the enemy on to attack was the second of the two subalterns of the detachment. It was difficult to believe that this usually shy and retiring young man could be the leader of a disloyal rising, but there he was, excitedly encouraging his followers to attack the house.

We hastily prepared lint and bandages

for the wounded, and watched with beating hearts the progress of the fight.

Suddenly, both sides ceased firing, the leaders advanced towards one another, conversed amicably together, evidently settled their differences, summoned their troops, and marched them home to breakfast. It was a sham fight.

This appears to be the favourite amusement of the officers who form the military element of Remyo society.

I was continually finding myself in the midst of desperate encounters when taking my rides abroad. It was rather disconcerting at first, but I grew accustomed to it in time, as one grows accustomed to anything, and would ride along the line of fire, with a coolness and indifference worthy of one of the old seasoned campaigners.

I suppose to those who live in a military district, sham fights are ordinary affairs, but I had never seen one before, and it struck me as very ludicrous to see these men, in most desperate earnestness, crouching in ambush, dodging behind trees, and crawling along under cover to escape the fire of their foes. The little Goorkhas become wildly excited, and it would not do to allow the two sides to come to close quarters, or the sham fight might develop into a real one.

The other European male inhabitants of Remyo, are the inevitable Indian Civilian and "Bombay Burman," whom of course I should not presume to analyse; two railway men (who seem superfluous as there is as yet no railway), a P. W. D. (Public Works Department) man, whose work, it seems, is to make roads (from my point of view as a cyclist they don't do him credit), an Engineer, and the Policeman.

This last was a mighty shikarri, who had hunted and shot every imaginable animal; who knew the habits and customs of all the beasts of the jungle, and after examining a "kill" would give a whole history of the fight between the tiger and its victim. He was a mighty talker too, and would converse for hours on any subject.

What he could not accomplish was to speak for three minutes without giving way to exaggeration ; nor could he give an unvarnished reply to a plain question, so that in Remyo " if you want to know the time *don't* ask a policeman " is the popular aphorism.

The Engineer possessed the most striking characteristics amongst the men of the place. I have never met a man so full of information. He was one of those men who can give information on every conceivable subject, for if he knows nothing about it, he will invent a few facts on the spur of the moment, facts of which he is always justly proud.

I never quite made up my mind whether his actions were the outcome of a passion for practical joking, or a desire to be of use, but I try to believe the latter. When I punctured my bicycle tyre he insisted upon helping me to mend it. His process occupied the whole of an afternoon, and the front veranda and drawing-room ; beyond this, it was too intricate to describe, except to say that it required all the available tooth brushes in the house, three basins of water, and a rupee piece, and necessitated, apparently, the cutting of a large hole in the inner tube, with a patent tyre remover he had invented out of a broken teaspoon.

On another occasion, he assured us he had a splendid plan for preventing our drawing room stove from smoking. We had been obliged to put a stove in the drawing room to make up for the absence of a fire place ; it was a primitive affair, with a chimney that went through a hole in the wall, and it smoked "somethink hawful." Our friend tried his plan and a dozen others, each more wonderful and complicated than the last, and each necessitating fresh holes in the already perforated wall. Each plan too, resulted in increased volumes of smoke, and as the furniture and carpet were being rapidly ruined, and our whilom happy home was being broken up, we finally remedied the matter ourselves.

But the matter wherein our Engineer excelled himself, was in the matter of rose trees.

Hearing us one day express a wish for a rose garden, he declared at once that nothing was easier. He was departing for Rangoon in two days, and he would there procure and send to us rose cuttings, which we must plant in carefully prepared boxes of soil, follow the instructions which he would give us concerning their welfare, and we should soon have flourishing rose trees. Our gratitude was unbounded, we listened and carefully noted his instructions, and after his departure eagerly awaited the fulfilment of his promise.

In a few days a coolie delivered at our house, what I took at first to be twigs for fire wood, but on examining the letter accompanying them, I discovered they were the promised rose cuttings. I felt some doubts about them, but my sister had implicit faith in the Engineer (the stove incident came later), and would not listen to me.

So we planted the rose cuttings, and for six whole weeks did we tend them. All the instructions we carried out to the letter, watering twice daily and sheltering them from the sun by day, and from the cold dews by night, but all to no avail. Dead sticks they were, and dead sticks they remained, till at last convinced of the hopelessness of attempting to restore life to the withered things, we tore them up in desperation and burnt them.

My sister's faith in the Engineer, however, remained still unshaken, and she protested that the coolie must have lost the original bundle of rose cuttings, and substituted these twigs in their place. For my part I believe no such thing, and when I consider what passionate care and tenderness we lavished on those unresponsive pieces of wood, I do indeed feel disposed to "speak with many words."

Varied though the characters and interests of the Remyo inhabitants may be, in one particular they all agree, i.e. in their dislike of the Casual Visitor.

The casual visitor is supposed to ruin the servants, to monopolise the tennis courts, and golf links, to abuse the privileges of honorary membership of the

club, to unjustly criticise the polo ground,
and generally to destroy the peace and
harmony of the station.

For the men, the advent of a lady
visitor means calls, dinner parties, and the
necessity of wearing best clothes, which
fills them with horror. For the ladies, it
means the advent of one who will possess
the latest fashions from Rangoon (possibly
from England), who will throw into the
shade their gala costumes of the fashion
of two years ago, who will trespass upon
their prerogatives, rival their powers at
tennis and golf, and generally interfere
with their peaceful and innocent pursuits.

The arrival of visitors, therefore, is not
welcomed as a rule, and though hospitably
received and comfortably housed, they are
not admitted into the inner life of the station
until they have shown themselves quite
innocent of the evil qualities which are
imputed to them.

This unexpected unfriendliness on the
part of the Remyoans has been brought
about by the acts of two people, who
once visited this happy valley, and

departed again leaving deeply rooted indignation behind them. Of the first, a woman, it suffices to say that she amply justified the suspicions of the Remyo ladies. Her name is never mentioned by them without a significant look, and she is not a safe subject for discussion.

The crime of the second sinner against Remyo hospitality (a man) was of a different nature, and it is perhaps difficult for the female mind to grasp the enormity of the offence.

A large tiger had made its appearance in the neighbourhood, and a tiger shoot had been organised. All the arrangements were complete; the men were sure of success, and speculated which of their number would have the luck to kill. The evening before the shoot, a visitor on his way from a remote station, arrived in Remyo, and obtained permission to accompany the sportsmen. As he was reputed to be a very bad shot this was readily given, and there was allotted to him a position well out of the expected line of the beat. The tiger broke near the stranger's tree, and he killed it with his first shot, the promoters of the shoot never even getting a sight of the game.

The criminal impertinence of a mere stranger daring to kill *their* tiger roused the deepest feelings of indignation among the Remyoans. The laws of hospitality are above all, so the perpetrator of the crime was allowed to escape with his life and the tiger skin, but since that day strangers have been looked upon as suspicious interlopers, and prospective tiger shoots are not discussed in presence of the Casual Visitor.

I have given my impressions of the Remyo society candidly, perhaps a little too candidly ; but lest any who read this book be disposed to hold the latter opinion, let me say one thing more.

The first, the last, and the most indelible impression left on my mind by all the Anglo-Burmans whom I had the pleasure of meeting, was the impression of a kindness, friendliness, and hospitality passing belief. The Anglo-Burmans, while retaining the best qualities of the English nation, seem to lose entirely that cold and suspicious reserve towards strangers, of which we are often so justly accused. They appear to have adopted those Eastern laws of hospitality, which lay so great a stress on the duty of entertaining strangers, and they cannot do enough to welcome those fellow countrymen who visit the land of their exile.

This characteristic kindness of the Anglo-Burmans is so universally acknowledged, that it is really superfluous to mention it, but as I spent six months among them, without encountering a single unkind look, word, or deed, I cannot let the opportunity pass without offering my tribute of gratitude to this most kind-hearted and generous people.

Chapter VII.

THE BURMESE.

"We are merry folk who would make all merry as ourselves."—"Yeomen of the Guard."

On my first evening in Remyo I was sitting in the drawing-room, waiting for the announcement of dinner, when suddenly, the curtain across the doorway was pulled aside, and a native peered into the room. His movements were rapid and stealthy, and betokened a desire for escape or concealment. On seeing me he slipped past the curtain into the room, and crouched down, as tho' endeavouring to hide himself from without. Then in the same bending attitude, he glided past the uncurtained window, across the room where I sat lost in astonishment, and on reaching my chair, sank on to his knees, placed his raised hands together in a supplicating manner, and exclaimed in a deferential and prayerful voice "Sarsiar." !

For a moment I stared at him in wonder, unable to comprehend his attitude ; and then in a flash I understood all.

He was in terrible danger, someone was pursuing him ; to escape he had slipped into the house, and was now imploring me to conceal or to defend him. I had no thought of hesitation, whatever might be his crime he must not be left to the rough justice of his pursuers, he must be protected until the matter could be properly inquired into.

I sprang up and hurried to the window to reconnoitre ; four natives stood in the road ; no one else was in sight ; perhaps the pursuers were already in the house.

"Sarsiar, sarsiar, thekinma," he repeated, (or something that sounded like that).

" All right, all right " I said soothingly : "don't be frightened, you're safe here," and so saying I quietly bolted the outer door, fastened the windows, and proceeded to put the room in a state of defence. My presence of mind evidently astonished him, he stared at me a moment and once more took up his cry of " Sarsiar, sarsiar,'

"It doesn't matter though a dozen Sarsiars are after you, "I cried impatiently : "you are quite safe here ; so tell me who is this "Sarsiar," and what have you done to him ?"

But the wretched man only became still more excited, he crouched lower than ever, he waved his arms, and burst into a torrent of Burmese eloquence, in which again and again, occurred the name of his pursuer, of this much dreaded "Sarsiar."

At last, being quite unable to either comprehend or calm him, I called aloud to my sister to come and reassure him in his own tongue. She came, exchanged a few hurried remarks with the fugitive, and then, to my utter astonishment and indignation, burst out laughing. I angrily demanded an explanation, and when she had recovered, she gave it.

The native was no terrified victim, flying from a savage foe, but the head boy announcing that dinner was ready !

The stealthy walk, the crouched air of concealment, the supplicating attitude, were merely expressions of respect, it being quite contrary to the Burman's idea of politeness to raise his head above that of his master.

This excessive politeness on the part of the Burman is highly commendable, but apt to be inconvenient. It is embarrassing to be waited on by a man who persists in scuttling about with his body bent almost double, and who sinks on his knees on every available occasion; it gives him an air of instability. Some were so full of respect as to dismount from their ponies and walk past the "Thekins" when they met us in the road. It must delay business immensely, but no true Burman would allow himself to be influenced by such a minor consideration.

The Burman is much given to contemplation. He is frequently seized with a fit of meditation in the midst of most important work, and will sit for hours, immovable, gazing steadily into vacancy, puffing at his huge cheroot, and thinking.

So, history relates, did Socrates sit for three days and nights, but Socrates, poor man, had no cheroot to soothe him.

J

The results of Socrates' meditation on that particular occasion are unknown ; so too are the results of the rapt meditations of the Burman. Never by word or deed does he betray what thoughts occupy his mind on these ever recurring occasions, but someday, who knows ? he may be moved to speak, and then where will be the wisdom of the East and of the West, when compared with the wisdom of this contemplative nation ? Surely it will become small and of no account, and be no more thought on !

For these fits of meditation are undoubtedly inspired ! They may overtake him at any time, absorbingly, unexpectedly, in a manner highly inconvenient to all with whom he may come in contact.

I say he is liable continually to such attacks, but certain surroundings, and circumstances seem more conducive than others to such contemplative meditation.

For example, if despatched on an important message, such an attack almost invariably seizes him, and the messenger will remain for hours, seated by the road side lost in thought, while his impatient master sits raging and fuming at home, waiting in vain for an answer to his note. On such an occasion the Burman loses all sense of time, and his expression of naive astonishment, and patient martyr-like sufferance, when blamed for his delay, is utterly disarming.

Again, the dusting of a room is most conducive to meditation. I have frequently seen a native stand for half an hour or more, immovable, duster in hand, gazing from the window, lost in abstraction. But this trait, I am told by English housewives, is not confined to Burmese servants alone. Dusting, I conclude, has a soothing effect on the nerves.

When the Burman does work, he works with an energy and violence which is as astonishing as it is unnecessary. To see a loogalay in his energetic movements, dusting or tidying a room is a lesson to sluggards.

He takes his stand in the centre of the room, and performs a series of wonderfully intricate and far reaching flag signals with the duster.   Then, after clearing away the broken china and other debris, he slowly makes a tour of the room, striking violently at each article of furniture once or twice with the corner of the afore-mentioned duster, and shaking the same menacingly in the face of every picture and ornament. Then he turns upside down the books and papers, carefully hides his mistress's work bag, and his master's favourite pipe, re-arranges the furniture and the ornaments, which have come through scatheless, to suit his own taste, and the room is finished. In the matter of floor washing the Burman as a rule prefers to carry out the precepts stated in Mr. Chevallier's song : "What's the good of anything ? Why nothing." To him it appears an act of supererogation to wash to-day the floor, which must certainly be dirtied again on the morrow.

But if he be induced, by the stern commands of his mistress to undertake the task, then indeed is it a day of mourning and discomfort for the whole household. No spring cleaning carried on by the most uncompromising and unsympathetic British matron, can approach the misery and upset caused by Burmese floor washing. ·

Every male member of the establishment, from the coolie who is mending the compound path, to the head boy, is recruited to the work, and reinforcements of " brothers " from the village are called in to assist. Every piece of furniture in the place is turned upside down, and then large cans of water are upset " promiscuous like " here and there, until the whole house is deluged. This accomplished, the concourse of servants commences to paddle about the house, rescuing books and cushions from the ravages of the flood, and flapping at the water with cloth and brooms. No definite scheme is adopted, but the chief idea seems to be to wet as much of the floor, walls, and furniture as possible. After this amusement has been pursued for about three hours, the floods are swept away through the drawing-room and out at the front door, and the damp and exhausted servants, after proudly announcing : " Floor much clean now, missis," retire triumphant, to rest their weary limbs for the remainder of the day. We did not often indulge our desire for cleanliness in this respect.

The Burman is a great lover of ceremonies and processions. On certain festival days long picturesque pageants wind thro' the villages on their way to the pagodas ; cart after cart drawn by gaily decorated bullocks and filled with brightly dressed occupants, many of whom wear fancy disguises, and dance and posture during the whole of the ride.

It is a strange sight to see "grave and reverend seigneurs" from the village, arrayed in the most extraordinary costumes, reminding one of an English Guy Fawkes procession, standing at the front of a cart, posturing and pulling faces, in a manner that would be ludicrous, were it not so evidently full of meaning and solemnity. Imitation boats, dragons and beasts of all sorts take part in these processions, which for grotesqueness, brilliance of colour, and originality of arrangement are equalled only in a Drury Lane pantomime or the Lord Mayor's Show. But the soul of the Burman is not satisfied with his great half yearly festivals, nor even with the smaller festivities that take place at every birth, wedding, death, "ear-boring," or other ceremonious occasion. He seeks ever for other opportunities for procession and masquerade.

Our Burmese servants found vent for their feelings in waiting at table. They performed their duties with as much stateliness and ceremony as time, and our impatient appetites would permit.

No dish, plate, or spoon was brought without the co-operation of the three loogalays who were in attendance, and the lord chamberlain himself could not have conducted the course of the meal with more dignity than did our Burmese butler.

But the greatest triumph was achieved at breakfast time when we partook of boiled eggs. The clink of the cups, followed by a hush of expectancy heralded what was coming. The purdah would be drawn aside by an unseen hand, and the procession would march solemnly into the room, the three loogalays, one behind the other, bearing each in his hand a very large dinner plate, in the centre of which stood a small egg in its humble egg-cup.

Into the room and round the table they would march, then dividing, each with a bow deposited his precious burden before the person for whom it was intended, after which the procession was again formed, and disappeared slowly behind the curtain: all this with an air of solemnity and display that would not have disgraced a royal levee. Why this ceremony was confined to eggs, why the porridge and bacon were not equally favoured I cannot tell, I merely state the facts as I observed them, leaving the explanation to others more discerning than I.

The greatest treat our own loogalays ever enjoyed in this respect was brought about one day by a slight mistake I made in giving an order to Po-Sin, the head butler. My grasp of the language being but slight, my speech was often a trifle faulty, but I gave orders with a vigorous confidence, and aided by gesture and "pigeon English"

I imagined that I made myself tolerably comprehensible. On the occasion to which I refer, I had prepared my sentence elaborately, and summoning Po-Sin, I informed him that his master would be at home and would want tea at three o'clock. There must have been some mistake somewhere. Possibly, I confused the word meaning ''office'' with the Burmese for ''three o'clock.'' But whatever be the explanation, about a quarter of an hour later, chancing to look out of the window, I beheld a procession winding its way along the road to the Court House, and bearing with it our afternoon tea equipage displayed to the highest advantage. At the head marched Po-Sin, proudly brandishing the teapot, then Po-Mya bearing the muffins, Po Thin with the tray and tea-cups, and behind, in regular order, the other numerous members of our establishment, each bearing some dish, jug, or spoon. They had gone too far to be overtaken, tho' they walked with becoming dignity, so with deep foreboding, I watched them disappear round the corner of the road leading to the Court House.

Presently I saw the disconcerted procession returning, headed this time by my infuriated brother-in-law, who had been interrupted in the midst of an important case, by the solemn entrance of the tea bearers. The servants looked depressed and disappointed. I think they had hoped the procession might be a weekly affair. Like "Brer Rabbit," I prudently lay low until my brother's wrath had exhausted itself.

The Burman has the reputation of being a keen sportsman, and certainly, his excitement is intense on every sporting occasion, especially in games of strength and skill. But he does not excel in these. His intentions are doubtless good, but he lacks pluck and determination.

This is especially evident when a loogalay fields for his master at cricket. He will watch the game with deepest interest, loudly applauding every hit, and when the ball speeds in his direction his excitement and pride are unbounded. He runs to meet it with outstretched arms, shouting wildly, then, as the ball nears him, and the audience hold their breath, expecting a wonderful catch or piece of fielding, he quietly steps aside, allows the ball to fly past him, and then trots gently after it, overtaking it some few yards over the boundary. His fellow natives view the performance with pride, and yell with admiration when he finally secures the ball and, carrying it within an easy throwing distance of the pitch, rolls it gently back to the bowler.

The interest taken by the natives in football is overpowering, and a spectator has been known to stick a knife into the calf of one of the most active of the players on the opposing side, who happened to be standing near the "touch line." A new and unexpected source of danger in the football field.

The two chief drawbacks to the Burman servant are, firstly, his intense self-satisfaction and conceit, and secondly, his intolerable superstition.

It is impossible to find fault with a Burman. He receives all complaints with a look of such absolute astonishment and reproach that the complainant is at once disarmed. In his own eyes the Burman can do no wrong, and if other folk do not entirely concur in this opinion, that is their misfortune and not his fault. He is always quite pleased with himself, and regards with a pitying contempt all who are not equally so.

Overpowering superstition is a deeply rooted characteristic of the race, and I rather suspect, a very convenient one occasionally. The Burman will do nothing on an unlucky day or hour, and in awaiting the propitious moment, the duty is frequently left undone altogether. This is apt to be inconvenient to others, if the duty in question be the delivery of an important message, or the preparation of dinner. But I have sometimes wondered whether this particular superstition might not advantageously be introduced into England, where it would be so exceedingly useful to the school boy at the end of the holidays, and to many other folk besides.

In private life the Burman carries his superstition to a ridiculous extent. No ceremony can take place, no festival be held, the building of a house cannot even be commenced until the wise man has declared the hour and place to be propitious.

All sorts of magical contrivances to prevent the entrance of wicked "nats" and other evil spirits, are erected outside nearly every house and village, and charms and horoscopes are believed in absolutely by all save the best educated Burmans.

They are a fickle people. Their lives being uneventful they love to vary them by constant small changes, and to enliven them by the excitement of gambling, which is the great vice of the country. We had a Burmese maid who displayed this love of change to a most astonishing degree. After being with us about two months she suddenly announced one morning that she had fever and must go and rest. Accordingly she disappeared for several days, and when we sent to enquire after her we learnt that she had recovered from her attack of fever, but was coming back to us no more, as she had got married. In about a fortnight she reappeared, saying calmly that she was now tired of being married, and was quite ready to return to her work after her little change.

Though he strongly objects to work himself the Burman likewise objects to see anyone else work. Whenever I endeavoured to clean my bicycle, our loogalays were terribly grieved. They sought me out in the quiet corner to which I had retired, and stood round me with the most shocked expressions, waving brooms and dusters, and beseeching me by all their most expressive gestures to leave the task to them. Sometimes they embarrassed me so much by all these attentions that I was obliged to consent, but always felt sorry afterwards; they are not satisfactory bicycle cleaners. The handle bars they polished again and again, but the rest of the machine struck them as uninteresting, and they left it severely alone.

My experience of the Burman was not confined altogether to our own servants, there were many in the village with whom I had a bowing acquaintance, but owing to my ignorance of the language I could

not hope to become intimate with them
and their families.

They appeared to take a great interest
in us and our possessions. Two little
Burmese ladies in particular, wives of the
chief men of the village, paid us constant
visits. They would bring us presents of
flowers and vegetables, offer these, and
then sit on the floor and stare resolutely
at us for the space of half an hour, at the
end of which time they would suddenly
make a profound obeisance and depart.

Conversation was impossible, as neither
party knew the other's language, but we
found this silent contemplation so embarrassing, that, after enduring it twice, we
endeavoured on the third visit to entertain
them by showing them pictures, trinkets,
or anything we thought might amuse them.
But with no great success; they admired
the things and then immediately returned
to their former occupation of staring, until
at last I thought of the piano (which at
that time was still in a healthy condition),
opened it, and began to play. That
interested them immensely, as they could

not understand whence the sound came. They would stand happily for any length of time, gingerly striking a note, and listening to the tone with the greatest wonder and delight.

But what pleased them more than any-thing was a china doll, belonging to my little niece, which shut and opened its eyes. Such a marvel had never been seen before, and the day after our visitors had discovered it, a large deputation from the village waited upon us, with a request to see the wonder. As from that time the doll frequently dis-appeared for a day or two, we rather suspected the ayah was turning an honest penny, by borrowing it to hire out for exhibition at various villages round, whither the rumour of its fame had already spread.

Our visitors took the greatest interest in our garments, and when their first shy-ness had worn off, would subject our costumes to a minute examination that was a little trying.

They always arrayed themselves in their

best garments when they came to see us, and very dainty they looked in their bright dresses of pink, green, or yellow silk, with flowers and ornaments in their black hair. The Burmese ladies are deservedly described as charming, and they understand the art of dress, and blending colours to perfection. They are reported to be very witty and amusing, as well as charming in appearance, and certainly when my brother happened to be at home on the occasion of their visits, they chattered to him very merrily, and seemed to thoroughly enjoy their talk with an Englishman.

Another visitor of ours was the thugyi, (the head man of the village), a very fine looking old man with one of the handsomest heads I have ever seen. He was taller than the majority of Burmans, and in the flowing white garments which he always wore, presented a splendid picture which I longed to paint. His manners were stately and dignified, and he treated us with the most royal courtesy, as though

K

he were an emperor at least.

The chief hpoongyi (priest) of Remyo was a dear old man, with a beautifully tender expression. At his invitation we all went to visit him one day, and he showed us over the kyaung, with its numerous images, bell, and quaint pictures of saints and devils. He was an enthusiastic gardener and showed us proudly over his domain, giving us much advice on the management of plants, and offering to transplant anything we admired to our own garden. A hpoongyi's life must be very peaceful and happy, though perhaps a trifle dull. His chief occupation seems to be meditation, which to us western folk appears distinctly monotonous.

Visits to the native bazaar afford endless amusement. Natives of all descriptions are gathered there, and the scene is most varied. The picturesque Burmans, giggling Chinese, chattering Madrassees, stately Parsees, solemn-faced Shans, and many other nationalities, swarm in the narrow streets and round the stalls of the bazaar. The stalls are large platforms raised about three feet from the ground, with over-hanging roofs. The seller sits in the middle of his stall with his wares spread round him, and keeps up a running flow of conversation the whole day long.

There never appeared to be much to purchase in the Remyo bazaar except a few silks and the most unpalatable looking foods, but I delighted to go there in order to watch the people. " Bazaar day," to the Burman is one big joke, and he enjoys it thoroughly. The girls wear their most becoming costumes, and seated in the midst of their lovely silks, form a picture dainty enough to attract any man's attention. They are charming, and are quite aware of the fact.

I ventured down once or twice to the bazaar with my camera, but they did not understand it, and regarded me with suspicion ; indeed, the mother of one little Shan laddie, whose picture I wished to take, worked herself up into such a state of wrath and terror that I was obliged to desist. I fancy she thought I was bewitching the poor little fellow.

My private opinion is, that in revenge
for my attempt on her son, she must have
induced one of their wise men to curse my
kôdak, for though I took photographs with
great vigour and confidence during my
travels, not a single one of them developed.
It is a singularly distressing employment
to sit long hours in a stuffy dark room,
developing photographs which steadily
refuse to develop.   I have met with many
sad experiences in my long and chequered
career, but I think this was the most
disappointing.

My one attempt at shopping by gesture
in the bazaar was not an unqualified
success.   I selected an aged and kindly
looking stall keeper, and proceeded to
collect together in a heap the few small
articles I desired to purchase.   During this
proceeding she watched my actions with
astonishment and some suspicion, but the
latter feeling was set at rest when I
produced a rupee and offered it to her.
She took it, and while she sought the
change, I pocketed my purchases.

NATIVE BAZAAR AT REMYO

But when she returned, her face expressed the greatest consternation, and she burst into a torrent of Burmese. Quite at a loss to understand her, I hurriedly offered her more money, but she refused it with scorn, and continued her explanations and entreaties, in which the numerous spectators of the scene presently joined, laughing as though it were the greatest joke in the world.

Presently the old lady picked up a bobbin of cotton, such as I had just bought, and waved it frantically in my face; I mechanically took it and pocketed it also. At this action on my part the spectators became still more hilarious, but the old lady looked annoyed, evidently considering the matter was getting beyond a joke.

At last, in desperation, I pulled out all my purchases and flung them on the stall. To my astonishment this proved to be precisely what she desired; the good lady beamed with satisfaction, gathered them together with her own fair hands, and returned them, and my change, to me with many bows and smiles. I do not know to this day what was the reason of her excitement. Judging by the intense amusement it caused the spectators, I should say the story will serve as a popular after dinner anecdote for many generations of Burmans.

I do not think anyone but a Burman could find much amusement in their dearly beloved Pwés. The dances, composed entirely of posturing and grouping, are most monotonous, and the music is distinctly an unpleasant noise from a European point of view. Yet these easily satisfied folk crowd to such entertainments (which occasionally last many days) and camp out round the temporary building in which they are performed. They seem to derive the greatest enjoyment from watching these interminable performances, following the inevitable dramatic "Prince and Princess" through their adventures, and chuckling over the vulgar jokes of the clown.

The Burman loves to laugh. He is as equally amused at a fire or a drowning fatality in real life, as when in the play the clown trips up a fellow actor.

His proneness to laughter is annoying sometimes, especially if one misses a drive at golf, or falls down stairs (either of which misfortunes appear to him very droll) but on the whole his keen appreciation of "humour" helps him very comfortably through life.

We modern Europeans may think we have a higher sense of humour than these simple folk ; but who is to judge ?

The Burman is, perhaps, after all that truest philosopher who finds latent humour in all things, and makes the most of it— still, I pray that, for his sake, his keenness of appreciation may not become more highly developed, or some day he will meet a pun, and it will kill him.

CHAPTER VIII.

—

ENTERTAINING.

"Thou didst eat strange flesh
Which some did die to look on."

—

Entertaining is nervous work, as all the world knows. The anxiety is considerably increased in a small country station like Remyo, because one cannot be sure that the rats will not devour the food beforehand, or that the cook will not take that opportunity of having "fever," a polite synonym for getting drunk, much in use among Burman servants.

The dinner party is the most general form of entertainment in Remyo, but not of very frequent occurrence; the reasons being, the limited number of available guests and the restricted nature of the menu. No sane person would dream of inviting another sane person to dine upon nothing but Burmese chicken, even displayed in various disguises from soup to savoury

Once a week beef can be obtained, so dinner parties are usually given on " beef days." Should an invitation arrive for another date, great excitement prevails as to what special delicacy has been procured.

Once we were presented with a peacock, and gave a dinner party to celebrate the event, the peacock itself being the chief item of the celebration. Our guests arrived full of anticipation of some unknown treat; we received them "big with pride."

But alas ! the vanity of human hopes. During the early part of the dinner, over the chicken entrées, the conversation turned upon the relative merits as food of various kinds of fowl. One of our guests, a man full of information on every subject, interesting and otherwise, suddenly announced cheerfully :

"One bird I may tell you is not fit for human food, and that bird is a peacock."

Thereupon ensued an awful pause, in the midst of which the servants entered, carrying the peacock in all its glory.

Nothing could be done. The bird was shorn of its tail, so to relieve our guest's mind we alluded to it as "goose," but no one could have been for an instant deceived. And the worst of it was, our guest was quite right, it was not fit for human food.

Another source of anxiety on giving a dinner party in Remyo is the decoration of the table. A Burmese loogalay has his own ideas about table decorations, and these ideas he will carry out, even if to do so obliges him to leave all his other work undone. In vain we may try to explain that we prefer to arrange the flowers ourselves, he looks pained, waits till we have completed our arrangements and have retired to dress, and then pounces upon the table and places his own elaborate decorations on the top of what we fondly imagined a triumph of artistic arrangement.

And his decorations are indeed elaborate; round every piece of glass, china, or cutlery he weaves a marvellous pattern, sometimes in bits of bracken, sometimes in coloured beads or rice, and occasionally in rose petals. When all is finished, the table looks like a kaleidoscope, and one is afraid to move a spoon or glass lest the design be destroyed.

On Christmas eve a large and important dinner party was given by some old inhabitants of the station. All the Europeans were invited, and it was intended that the evening should be spent in jovial and merry games like a typical Christmas eve at home. But alas! never was an entertainment beset with greater difficulties.

In the first place, nearly all the guests upon whom we most depended for amusement sent word that they had fever. We suspected that fever at the time, and suspected it still more next day, when we heard of a jovial bachelor gathering that same evening in the house of one of the stricken ones.

Then the weather was not cheering. It was a terribly cold night, and the houses in Remyo, being mostly of Government design, consequently the same for both hills and plains, are not calculated to keep out the cold; there are large chinks in the unpapered walls, and few of the doors and windows will shut. In this particular house there was no fire place, only a small stove which gave out about as much warmth as a spirit kettle. We all felt grateful to our host and hostess for their hospitality, and did our best to be entertained and entertaining in our turn, but it is hard to keep up a cheerful appearance and jovial spirits, in evening dress, in a mat house, with no fire and the temperature almost down to freezing point.

We played games such as "Kitchen Furniture" and "Family Post" which necessitated plenty of movement, and gave every one in turn an opportunity of occupying the chair by the stove.

That part of the evening which I enjoyed most was when I made the mulled claret. I had no idea how to make it, but I should obtain uninterrupted possession of the stove during the operation, so I volunteered for the task. I put the claret, and anything suitable and "Christmassy," I could think of, into a saucepan, and stirred it over the stove until the other guests became suspicious, and I was forced to abandon my warm post.

I did not like the result at all, and I noticed the other guests lost interest in it as a drink after the first sip, though they clung to their glasses, using them as impromptu hand warming pans.

But what proved the greatest check upon the enjoyment of the evening was the great anxiety of the guests for the welfare of the furniture.

Our host and hostess were on the point of leaving the station, and as is the custom, had sold their furniture to the other residents, though they retained it in their house until departure. Now when one has just bought, and paid for, say, a set of drawing room chairs, or china ornaments, one does not enjoy seeing the former subjected to the rough usage of a game of "Bumps" nor the latter endangered by a game of Ball. Consequently, each and all were busily engaged during the evening in protecting their prospective possessions, and had little opportunity of abandoning themselves to enjoyment.

One very amusing instance of this was the behaviour of the new owners of the carpet. It was a poor carpet, old, faded, and thread-bare, but it was the only carpet in the station and the recent purchasers regarded it with pride. They looked anxious all the evening, when chairs were dragged about over weak spots, and peg glasses were placed in dangerous proximity to restless feet.

But the climax of their concern was reached when "Snap dragon" was proposed. The game was hailed with delight by every one (there really is a little imaginary warmth in the flame), but the contempt of the carpet-owners was unbounded. They said nothing, but looked volumes; they did not join in the game, but crawled about the ground round the revellers, busily engaged in picking up the numerous raisins scattered on the floor, forcibly holding back feet which threatened to crush the greasy fruit, and showing by all means in their power that they considered "Snap dragon" a most foolish amusement.

Small wonder, considering all these disadvantageous circumstances, that the Christmas party was not an unqualified success, and that the cold and weary guests, plodding home in the early hours of Christmas morning, mentally vowed that such wild dissipation was not good for them and should never again be repeated.

Dances are necessarily unknown in such a small station as Remyo. An energetic bachelor did once make an effort to give one, but as the only available room was the ticket office at the railway station, the only available music the bagpipes of the Goorkhas, and the only available ladies five in number, he was reluctantly obliged to abandon the project.

A much enduring form of entertainment in Remyo is the musical afternoon, or evening party. The inhabitants assemble in turns at one of the three houses which boast a piano ; but the repertoire of the combined station is limited, and as every one expects to sing on these occasions (ignorance of time and tune being considered no drawback), and further, intends to sing one or other of the few songs most popular in the station, things are not in any sense as harmonious as they should be.

This great eagerness to perform entailed much manœuvring to obtain first possession of the piano, and it was amusing to watch the expressions of mingled indignation and scorn on the faces of others less fortunate, when they recognised the prelude to what they each claimed as their own particular song.

The singer's triumph, however, was not without compensating disadvantages, his efforts being assisted by a distinctly audible chorus in undertone which would cling to him throughout the song in spite of his endeavours to throw off the encumbrance by means of abrupt changes of tempo, and variations in the air ; and this professed appreciation of the performance evoked from the singer such gratitude as one would expect under the circumstances.

No ! On the whole we did not " entertain " much in Remyo ; we contented ourselves with quiet, domestic lives, enlivened but occasionally by such outbursts of wild revelry as I have described.

CHAPTER IX.

ADVENTURES.

"Things are seldom what they seem "—" H.M.S. Pinafore."
" I haven't braved any dangers, but I feel as if I
knew all about it "—(Rudyard Kipling.)

BUT all this time I am wandering from
the real subject of this book, *i.e.*, myself
and my adventures, and as wandering from
the straight path is an unpardonable error,
it behoves me to return speedily to my
subject, and recount a few of the soul-
stirring incidents which befell me during
some of my many bicycling expeditions
alone into the depths of the jungle.

This bicycling out of sight of human
habitation, into the depths of the jungle,
sounds rather a brave and fearless proceeding, so I will not correct the statement,
but in parenthesis, as it were, I will remark
that once only did I venture more than
half a mile from Remyo, and that whenever I had turned the corner of the
circular road, which shut out the last view
of my brother's house, my heart sank, and

I became a prey to the most agonising fears. Every instant I expected a tiger to bound upon me from the jungle at the side of the road, a cobra to dart out its ugly head from the overhanging branch of a tree, or a body of dacoits to pounce down upon me and carry me off to their lair in triumph. My mind was filled with useless speculation as to whether I and my bicycle would be swifter than a panther, and with what "honeyed words of wisdom" I should best allay the wrath of the "Burman run amuck," should fate throw one of these in my way.

I derived no pleasure from that lonely mile and a half of the circular road, which must be traversed before again arriving at the haunts of civilisation ; I never entered upon it without a shiver of nervous expectation, or left it behind without a sigh of relief, and yet I was forced by my overweening craving for adventure, to ride out at every opportunity to explore this dreary waste of jungle ! Like the great "Tartarin" of "Tarasconnasian" memory, my "Don Quixote" spirit drove

me to seek adventures, however gruesome,
while my "Sancho Panza" mind ever
timidly pined for home and safety.

The first time my Quixotic expectations
were fulfilled, was one evening when I
was riding later than usual. The sun had
set, and the short eastern twilight was
rapidly darkening into night.   I was
cycling along quickly, eager to reach home
before being overtaken by the gathering
darkness, when suddenly, on turning a
corner of the road, I saw, about a hundred
yards in front of me, a long black thing,
presumably a python, stretching half across
the road, and curving up its huge head, as
though ready to attack.

I do not suppose any bicycle ever stopped
so abruptly as mine did at that moment,
and I must confess that my descent from
the machine was rapid rather than graceful.

After I had sorted myself and the
bicycle, I stood up, my senses somewhat
steadied by the sudden contact with
mother earth, and considered the situation.
The python did not appear to have moved

much, and had, apparently, as yet taken no notice of my appearance ; could it be asleep ? I suppose pythons do sleep sometimes ?

If I turned back, behind me lay three miles and more of jungle bordered road, full of endless possible dangers, which must be traversed before reaching safety, and it was growing so dark. In front, if I could but pass the python, I had but a quarter of a mile to ride and I should be in Remyo. I felt that I positively dared not face that long, dark, ride back; but dare I face the python ? It still made no sign of movement; but possibly it was shamming sleep.

Then suddenly there came to me in my need, not a mysterious voice, but a timely recollection. It was a recollection of one of the stories told me by the versatile policeman; a story of how he had behaved successfully under similar circumstances, except that in his case the obstacle was a leopard. I determined to follow his example.

Summoning all my courage to assist me

in performing this fearsome deed, I mounted my bicycle, and with beating heart and trembling limbs, I rode straight towards the reptile, ringing my bell, shouting, and making as much noise and commotion as possible. Straight on I rode, almost desperate with fear,————and then suddenly I ceased to shout, I stayed my reckless pace, and finished my ride in gloomy silence, for on nearer inspection the mighty python, the object of all my terror, turned out to be nothing more alarming than the fallen branch of a tree.

Another adventure (which but for my habitual prudence might have ended more seriously) befell me at almost exactly the same spot, but in the day time. I was riding along cheerfully, feeling particularly brave, when suddenly I beheld about a quarter of a mile in front of me three strange beasts.

They rather resembled to my mind rhinoceri, but each had two horns. I had never seen them before (I have no particular desire ever to see them again) and I had not the least notion what they might be; whether wild beasts of the jungle or tame household pets, but their personal appearance rather suggested the former. I dismounted hastily, and considered the matter. I did not wish to appear cowardly, even to my bicycle; on the other hand, being of a peaceful nature, I had no desire to enter into a hand-to-hoof struggle with three utterly unknown quantities.

On they came, usurping the whole of the road, with a sort of "push-me-aside-if-you-dare" look about them, which I found particularly unpleasant. Their gait was rolling and pompous, but they occasionally relieved the monotony of their progress by prodding one another playfully with their horns. This engaging playfulness of disposition did not appeal to me.

But I remembered the python incident, and scorned my fears, I would go on and face the beasts. I remounted, looked again at the horns of the advancing animals, thought of my family and friends, and then, somehow, my bicycle seemed to turn round by itself, and I found myself speeding as quickly in the opposite direction as any record breaker who ever rode.

On arriving home, I casually mentioned what I had encountered, and learned that my friends were "water buffalos," animals of the mildest disposition unless roused, but when roused, most unpleasant to encounter. They have frequently been known to pick up a dog with their horns, and break its bones over their backs. They can pick a mosquito off their backs with the tip of their horns, in fact they are quite skilled in the use of the latter, and had I not luckily decided to ride in the opposite direction when I encountered these enterprising beasts, they would, doubtless, have experienced no difficulty whatever in puncturing my tyre!

Ostensibly, their duty in this life is to draw the plough, but in reality they fulfil a far higher mission. To them, and to them only, it is given to draw contempt upon the superiority of the Anglo Indian: to compass the fall of the mighty.

For no sooner does a European appear riding in his pride by the river bed, where the water buffalo lies wallowing in the mud, than all the worst passions awake in the breast of the afore mentioned water buffalo, and he is instantly aroused to anger. He leaves the delights of the mud bath, and starts in pursuit of the white face, no matter who he may be. "Tell it not in Gath" but the water buffalo, being no respecter of persons, has even been known to put to ignominious flight the "Indian Civilian" and the "Bombay Burman." The pursuit is long and determined, the attack almost inevitable, unless the pursued be rescued by the opportune advent of a native, for to the water buffalo the word of the Burman is law, while the word of the Anglo Indian is a mere nothing.

This then, "the scorning of the great ones," would seem to be the purpose of the water buffalos upon this earth. "How are the mighty fallen"! when the highest among the ruling race must trust for rescue to the interference of a five year old Burman.

One day, late in the afternoon, I sallied forth on my bicycle to a spot half a mile down the Mandalay road, where I had noticed a specially beautifully blossomed wild cherry tree. My intention was to rob the tree of its treasure, and bear the blossom home in triumph to decorate our drawing room for a dinner party that evening.

The place was quite deserted, so finding I could not reach the blossoms from the ground, I leant my bicycle against the tree trunk, and after much scrambling, and one or two falls, I succeeded in climbing the tree, and began to gather the flowers.

So absorbed was I in my two-fold task of holding on to my precarious perch, and breaking the branches of blossom, that I did not notice what was going on below. Imagine then my horror and astonishment, on looking down, to find my tree surrounded by about a dozen of the most extraordinary looking natives I had ever beheld. Their clothing was most scanty and they were covered from head to foot with elaborate "tattoo." They wore tremendously large Shan hats, their hair was long and matted, their teeth were red with betel juice, and most of them were armed with long Burmese "dahs" (knives). They had come silently along the road out of the jungle, and now stood in a circle round my tree, pointing, staring, and chattering vigorously in an unknown tongue.

Evidently I had fallen into the hands of a band of dacoits, and to judge by their appearance, they were gloating over their capture.

It was no dream this time—I assured myself of that by a series of violent and judicious pinches ; no ! it was grim, very grim, earnest. Escape appeared impossible. I told them in as much strong English as I could remember, to go away, but they neither understood nor heeded. I tried to recollect my Burmese, but could only remember words referring to food, and thought it better not to put that idea into their heads; they might be cannibals. I tried one or two shouts, but that made no impression on them. There seemed no hope ; they still stood there, pointing and grinning savagely; they had evidently no intention of relinquishing their prey.

Then, trying to smile in a nervous and conciliatory manner, I slowly descended the tree.   How I longed for false teeth, a glass eye, a wooden leg, or some other modern invention, with which people in books of adventure are wont to overawe the natives who thirst for their blood. Alas ! I had nothing of the sort.

I could not, obviously, sit in the tree all night, so sadly and doubtfully I descended to throw myself on their mercy.

I reached the ground, and stood with my eyes shut waiting the end.

The end showed no intention of coming, so I opened my eyes, and discovered to my astonishment that not I but my bicycle was the object of all this attention.   I was to them a matter of no interest whatever, but the cycle they could not understand.

Joyous with relief I hurriedly demonstrated the workings of my bicycle to this party of, not dacoits, but most harmless wood cutters, and then mounting rode away, followed for some distance by an awe-struck and admiring crowd.   My fears as usual were unfounded, but the drawing room was not decorated with cherry blossom that or any other evening.

It is difficult, for those to whom the bicycle is now as common as blackberries, to imagine the astonishment with which the natives view the machine for the first time. In Remyo itself bicycles were well known, but frequently on the roads I met strangers from neighbouring villages, and the astonishment and terror depicted on their faces when they beheld me riding on this unknown thing was almost laughable. They would fall back into the ditch with their mouths open, and remain staring after me as long as I was in sight.

Once, I remember, I and another lady rode out to a little village in the jungle about three miles from Remyo. The road, a mere jungle track, was awful, but we succeeded at last in arriving at our destination. We left our cycles in the compound of the "hpoongyi kyaung," and climbed a neighbouring hill to see a quaint pagoda, which crowned its top. After thoroughly examining the pagoda, and the numerous images which surround it, we returned to our cycles.

What was our astonishment to find the

entire population of the village assembled in the compound, all having apparently taken up their positions there, preparatory to seeing some entertainment. The Head of the village approached us humbly, and in a long speech explained that though he (evidently a travelled gentleman) had told his subordinates all about the wonderful machines we rode, yet they would not believe him. Would we, as a great condescension, mount and ride round the compound, that all might see that his words were true.

Willing to oblige him, I consented at once, mounted, and did a little "gymkhana business," rather cleverly, I thought, considering the rough ground. Imagine my astonishment and indignation, when the whole audience became convulsed with merriment, hearty, overwhelming merriment, rolling on the ground, and shrieking with laughter. I cannot explain the reason of it ; I suppose they looked upon me as a sort of travelling acrobat, and their laughter was a sign of approbation of my tricks. But I was very angry. I had not gone out to

Burmah to become the laughing stock of ignorant natives, so I said a hasty farewell to the "Thugyi," who seemed quite pleased with the reception his companions gave me, and rode out of the compound and away, followed by the amused shrieks of my audience. I would have shaken the dust of that village from my feet, but that is a difficult thing to achieve successfully on a bicycle.

The Burmans are a merry folk, but methinks at times their humour carries them too far.

CHAPTER X.

—

BEASTS AND REPTILES.

—

The animals came in one by one
Till Noah, he thought they would never have done.

And they all came into the Ark.
For to get out of the rain.

—

RATS ! Hamlin Town (with Bishop Hatto thrown in) cannot offer a comparison with our sufferings from these pestilent vermin.

During the day time they contented themselves with playing in twos and threes about the house, getting in the way of our feet, and generally making themselves a nuisance. But at night when we had retired to rest, they came in their hundreds, from their homes beneath the house, and to use an expressive Americanism "simply bought the place."

I am not naturally a "Mrs. Gummidge," but in this instance I am certain I suffered more than any others in Remyo.   Why the rats should have preferred my room I know not, but undoubtedly they did. They gave balls every night on my dressing table, and organised athletic sports, chiefly hurdle races, on the floor.   They had glorious supper parties on my trunks, leaving the whole place scattered with half-eaten walnuts, bits of biscuit, and morsels of cheese.   They had concerts and debating societies in the still hours of the night, brawls and squabbles at all times ; and true to tradition, made nests inside my Sunday hats, helping themselves to such of my finery as took their fancy.

As I have said, they came in their hundreds, and I was powerless against them.   In vain did I sit up in bed and "shoo" and clap my hands, they would pause for an instant, as the revellers in Brussels paused when they heard the cannon of Quatre Bras, then : "On with the dance let joy be unconfined, no sleep till morn when rats and walnuts meet," and

M

the noise would become more deafening
than ever.   I think they grew to enjoy my
"shooings;" " the more noise the merrier"
was evidently their motto ; but one night
when I dozed off after making myself particularly disagreeable, a large rat sprang
upon my pillow, tore aside the mosquito
curtains, and hit me violently with its tail.
They are revengeful creatures.

And what appetites they had ? Poison
they scoffed at, but ate everything else
that was not soldered up in tin boxes,
(from our Christmas pudding, to the Baby's
pelisses, and my best gloves). Their most
criminal act of depredation, was in regard
to my brother's pipe. It was a beautifully
grained pipe which I took out from England
for a Christmas present. On Christmas
Eve the rats penetrated into the drawer
where I kept it, tore away the wrappings,
and set to work. In the morning nothing
was left but the stem, the perforated and
jagged remains of the bowl, and a little
heap of chawed bits of wood. My brother
was very angry when I broke the news to
him, but it wasn't my fault, they were his

rats ; he ought to have had them under better control.

We got a dog, but he was useless. He was a pariah puppy, of respectable parents ; a cheery, popular fellow, who had so many evening engagements among his friends in the village, that he could scarcely ever spare a night at home ; and during the day time he mostly slept. My sister and I both disliked him, she because he *would* worry the Baby's legs, I because he developed such an unbounded devotion to my shoes.

He never attached himself to other shoes in this way, but mine he would not leave alone. He carried some off every day and hid them behind the furniture, or if he had a quiet ten minutes to himself, he buried them in the compound. Many a long lost shoe did we discover when turning out the drawing room, or digging up the flower beds. The others were amused at this frolicsome trait, but it was rather a stupid joke really.

I was assured by the inhabitants of Remyo that mosquitos are unknown there during the cold weather. If this be really the case, there must have been a special pilgrimage, and obviously I was the object of their attentions. Fresh from England, they welcomed me with a delight that ought to have been highly gratifying; nor could they do enough to show their unbounded appreciation of me. I obtained mosquito curtains, but I suppose I was clumsy in the manipulation of them, for I spent many a lively night in the company of two or three enthusiasts who kept me awake by their odious "ping-ping" song, and their still more odious attentions.

There is a district in Burmah, I am told, where the cattle are provided with mosquito curtains, and I can quite believe it, for if they can be so obnoxious in the hills in the cold weather, what must they be in the plains in the heat! All creatures have their work in this world, and I suppose the mosquito was created to subdue female vanity; one cannot well be vain with such a complexion as they gave me.

But let me quit this melancholy subject ; it is impossible to be jocular with a mosquito, and strong language would be out of place in this book.

Rats are not the only creatures in Remyo with whom we were forced to share our meals. The place abounds in ants, beetles, and " creeping things innumerable," and all these must live ; which necessity we recognised, but wished they could live elsewhere.

On the whole, I think the ant is the most objectionable of insects. There is a Burmese fable concerning an ant and a lion which tells how the ant was rewarded for assistance rendered to the lion, by receiving permission to go everywhere, and so that this prerogative may be fully exercised, the ant has, apparently, been gifted with matchless ingenuity in devising means to overcome all obstacles. Amongst other accomplishments it must have acquired the art either of swimming, flying or bridge building, for even the dishes of water, in the centre of which we placed our meals, were ineffectual.

The worthy Dr. Watts tells us to "go learn of the ant to be prudent and wise," but though it is with the most submissive humility that I venture to contradict such an authority on natural history as the gifted author of "How doth the little busy bee," yet I must confess that I do not recognise in the ants the first of the virtues indicated.   They devastated a full box of chocolates in a single night, which surely was hardly prudent, unless they possess iron constitutions.

It was without doubt profitable for us to have constantly before us the example of the clever and industrious ant, and we tried to profit thereby, but at times we could not help feeling that the sluggard would have been the more acceptable companion ; the ant is so painfully energetic, especially in the matter of absorbing food—the sluggard, I feel sure, had more regard for his digestion.

I never learned to distinguish the names of the innumerable crawling creatures whom we met at table at meal times.   Their sole characteristic is greed, and they kept me continually reminded of the plagues of Egypt, for they came in unlimited numbers, settling on the food, darkening the air with their numberless forms, and devouring everything eatable ! They are eminently objectionable, and I defy the most devout lover of natural history and "beasties" generally, to find any pleasure in their society.

One evening I was dining out, and towards the middle of dinner I perceived a large, hideous object nestling among the profuse flower decorations on the table. It didn't appear to me a very pleasant table companion, but as no one else remarked it, and as I dislike appearing disconcerted by the habits of strange countries, I said nothing about it so long as the creature remained quiet. But when at last it came out from its lair, and curling up its long tail made a run at me, I left the table hurriedly.

To my relief the other guests also displayed uneasiness, for the object of my dislike was a scorpion, which had, it was supposed, been brought into the room with the flowers, and had remained hidden from all eyes but mine until its unwelcome disclosure of itself. There ensued an exciting chase up and down the table after the animal, till it was at length caught between two table spoons and drowned in a finger bowl.

By little excitements of this kind the entertainments in Burmah are often enlivened. Some doubt has been cast upon this story by sceptical Europeans, but if any require proof, I can refer them to eminent members of the I. C. S., (men whom none would dare to doubt), who will assure them that such occurrences are frequent ; in fact that the first place one would look for a scorpion would be among the flowers upon a dinner table !

When watching the antics of a plump good tempered Jim Crow, as he disports himself upon a pleasant English lawn, or when listening to his peaceful " cawing " among the shady trees on a hot summer's day, one little dreams that this same harmless, law-abiding creature, when exposed to the degenerating influences of the east, becomes transformed into the most disreputable vagabond upon the face of the earth.

The impudent thefts by jackdaws have long been famed, but no words can describe the unbounded presumption of the Burmese crows.

They are always on the watch, and if food be left for an instant in a room with open door or window, they enter, and settle on the table without a moment's hesitation, helping themselves to anything that takes their fancy, in the coolest manner imaginable. When the loogalays carry the dishes of food from the kitchen to the house, these same impish crows pounce down on them and bear away any tempting morsels, well knowing that the men have their hands full, and cannot make reprisals. They appear to know by instinct the approach of meal times, and settle in crowds on the veranda rail or the window ledge, ready to carry off the food directly one's back is turned, and in the meanwhile they pull faces at us, and make rude remarks, for all the world like a collection of vulgar little street boys.

They know no fear; they only mock and mimic "shooings" and hand clappings, and would laugh, I am sure, at the most awe-inspiring scare-crow ever erected. They sometimes go so far as to deliberately settle on the table and take a peck out of the cake, while one is sitting there, and then before they can be caught, they give a cheeky "caw," bow ironically, and flutter back to rejoin their admiring comrades (who have doubtless dared them to the act) on the veranda. I do not believe there exists any other creature in the world possessed of such boundless cheek.

They have a strong sense of humour of a practical-joking kind, and one of their amusements in Remyo was to lure us away from the tea table by feigned attacks upon our pots of hyacinth bulbs, which they uprooted in the most devastating manner. We would fly out to the protection of our precious bulbs, and return to find our cakes devoured or carried away, by a reserve body of crows, who had been waiting in ambush behind the door.

They occasionally combine forces with other thieves. The most wearing half hour I ever spent was one devoted to protecting the interest of the cake and the cream jug, from the hostile attacks of half a dozen crows and two kittens. While I lifted down the latter from the table the former settled upon the cake, and when I turned my attentions to them, the kittens returned to the charge. Mercifully, allies are not usually forthcoming ; only young, ignorant, and disobedient kittens would associate with the disreputable crows ; all properly brought up birds and beasts avoid association with them. Even the vultures, who sat all day on the trees shading the hospital, were contemptuous of those wicked "gamin" the crows.

Dogs abound in every Burmese village, and they and the pigs are the chief scavengers of the place. Their number is legion, for it is contrary to the

Buddhist religion to take life, so all puppies are allowed to live ; and as it is further considered an act of merit to feed them, they have a fairly pleasant existence.

The pariah dog performs his scavenging duties conscientiously, but he possesses few other merits to recommend him to one's esteem. He is at best a stupid, noisy, thieving brute, whose "customs are nasty and whose manners are none ; " he occupies his time eating, sleeping, and fighting, and his chief amusement is to snap at the heels of the European, and lie across the road to upset the unwary bicyclist. Periodically, when the pest becomes unbearable, a day of slaughter is appointed by the Majesty of the Law, and all dogs who have no owner are poisoned. But in spite of this rigorous measure, there never seems much diminution in the numbers.

Our neighbour possessed three English dogs,—two terriers and a greyhound. They had, no doubt, been well brought up, but had been led astray by evil companions, and they joined in the campaign which the rats, crows, and other creatures carried on against us. They delighted to creep into our compound, trample on the flower beds, steal my cakes (perhaps the household was not altogether sorry for that), and make away with our tennis balls. One day, they drove a herd of ponies all over our beloved garden, and then retired chuckling, to watch from a safe distance, our desperate attempts to induce the bewildered creatures to find the gate.

The greyhound, I think, would have been a harmless creature, but the terriers possessed a full share of the devilry of their breed, and urged him to accompany them in all their audacious tricks. I believe it was they who persuaded three goats (the chief destroyers of our kitchen garden) to commence their raiding expeditions into our grounds, for the goats always appeared from the neighbourhood of the dog's kennels, and there was generally one terrier, at least, watching when Po Sin's energetic chase of the goats over the radish beds began.

Other animals there were in the neighbourhood of Remyo, dwellers in the jungle, very different from the mischievous crew I have just described. Tiger, bear, panther, cheetah, soft-eyed gyee, hares, jackals, and others. Sometimes, as night drew near, I tried to picture how the inhabitants of the jungle would be waking from sleep and preparing for their busy night's work.

The "Jungle Books" had of course inspired me with a great interest and affection for all these animals, especially "Baloo" the bear, and "Bagheera" the black panther, and I continued to love them so long as they remained at a respectable distance, but when, at times, they made expeditions into our neighbourhood, my admiration changed to awe.

A tiger was the first visitor; he killed two ponies in the stable of a neighbour. Then a black panther commenced to parade, nightly, the road between our house and the club. He snapped up a little terrier which was trotting along at its master's heels one evening; he was reported to have been seen many times

about dusk, slinking along by the road
side, and one man broke a record on his
bicycle, followed by an innocent and
admiring pariah dog which he mistook for
the panther. There is no doubt that the
panther really did for a time haunt the
road, but he was so useful as an excuse
for the men to stay late at the club till
they could get a lift down in someone
else's dog-cart (an excuse that appeared
quite convincing to their nervous wives)
that he almost became an institution.

From the first I distinctly disliked
jackals. My bedroom window opened upon
the back veranda, and one night I was
awakened by a noise, and looking out I saw
two of these beasts (I did not know at the
time what they were) walking softly up
and down devouring some food which the
loogalays had left there.

For some time I watched them, fascin-
ated by these shadowy dark forms creeping about in the moonlight. Then,
remembering that the back door was
unfastened, that I was most probably the
first person they would encounter should

they enter, and that I had promised faithfully to return to England in six months,
I thought it time to rouse my brother-in-
law.

Accordingly, I crept from my room,
wakened him and my sister, and told
them to get up, to bring their guns, and
follow me, as the back veranda was
full of wild animals, who might at any
moment break into the house. They were
both singularly uninterested in my information (indeed my brother only sleepily
murmured "let them break" and went to
sleep again) but I insisted, and at last he
rose in a very bad temper and came to
inquire into the cause of my alarm.

Of course, the noise he made tumbling
about and opening the door scared our
visitors, and when he went out, the veranda
was empty. A few scathing remarks
about my powers of imagination were all
the thanks I received for thus saving the
lives of the family. Ingratitude, thy
name is brother-in-law !

After that my visitors came frequently,
but I felt that I would rather die than risk

more sarcasm, and when I found they had no evil intentions I grew rather to enjoy watching them. Their marvellous quickness, their caution, and the silence of their movements seemed to give a faint suggestion of what jungle life must be, though, of course, the jackal compared with the nobler animals, is no more than "Jacala, the belly that runs on four feet."

After a while, our visitors were inspired to show their gratitude by nightly serenades. Gratitude is always delightful to meet with in man or beast, but I wished their's had taken some other form. A jackal's voice is powerful but unpleasant, and has a mournful effect upon the nerves.

Of dead beasts I saw many. The jungle round Remyo seemed to be a perfect menagerie, and a noble panther, tiger or bear was often borne in triumph into the station and deposited in the centre of the Club compound, to be admired of all beholders.

When no time could be spared for an

N

organised shoot, a reward would be
offered for the carcase of any panther or
cheetah which might have been annoying
a neighbouring jungle village, and the
animal, when killed, was always brought in
to be shown to my brother by the claim-
ants of the reward. It was a little
startling at first to have bears, panthers,
etc., casually brought and deposited at
one's front door, but we grew accustomed
to it after a while, as one grows accustomed to all things but hanging. On one
occasion some natives brought in the body
of a huge leopard which had killed and
eaten a man near their village (a most
unusual proceeding for a leopard), and a
terrible looking animal it was, with huge
claws and teeth, and a sneaking deceitful
face. The whole incident was disagreeably
gruesome.

On another occasion we were presented
with two live bear cubs, whose parents had
been killed. They were dear little fluffy
brown creatures, and we longed to keep
them, but they generally become a great
nuisance when older, as they are always

treacherous, and capable any day of trotting into the village and killing half a dozen people as a morning's amusement.

I was strangely lucky (or unlucky, I hardly know which to call it) in the matter of snakes, for I did not see a single live snake during my visit. I constantly expected to meet one in the compound or jungle, but I never even found one coming up the water-hole in the bath-room, or coiled up in my bed. The creatures never came near me, even though I spread out the skin of a huge rock snake in the compound, in the hopes that its relations (as is invariably the custom with snakes in books) might be induced to assemble.

The most wise looking creatures (always excepting the elephants) which I saw were the Burmese bullocks. Their grave, thoughtful, placid faces reminded me of the images of Gaudama. As they crawl along their way drawing the creaking bullock carts to the bazaar, or trot merrily through the jungle, taking gaily-attired Burmans to attend a Pwé, they have ever

the same patient, quiet, abstracted expression, as though this menial work is to
them a mere appendage to the deeper life
of meditation.   This is what their expression conveys to me; some think it denotes
stupidity.

The cattle belonging to the Burmese
appear to be most independent animals.
Each morning they wander away into the
jungle at their own sweet wills, returning
at night of their own accord for the milk-
ing.   We were much astonished one day,
when, in answer to our request that the
milk might be brought earlier in future,
the milkman replied with much "shekkohing" and humility that it could not be,
as the cow did not wish to return earlier
from her walk.   The Burmans are very
casual in their treatment and care of the
cattle, numbers of which fall victims to
tigers and other rapacious beasts.

This chapter would not be complete
without a word or two about the Burmese
ponies; but who am I, who never could
make head or tail of any pony's propensities,
to presume to describe their character?

Very small and wiry are they, very
devoted to polo (which they understand
quite as well as their masters, and which
they play with the same keenness) ; conceited and obstinate ; but obedient and
affectionate to their masters, and possessing as great a love of a joke as a Burman
himself.

One of our ponies, "Pearl," a lovely
little animal, and a splendid polo player,
possessed all these characteristics. With
her master or mistress she was as gentle
and submissive as anyone could desire, but
she assumed the most unpardonable airs
towards all the rest of the world. She
received caresses and attentions with a
haughty disdain, turned up her nose at
any but the very best food, and led her
poor sais a most trying time. I admired
her from afar, but we never became intimate ; she evidently despised me, and had
the most disagreeable knack of making me
feel ignorant and small. She was too
much of a lady to show her dislike by
kicks or snaps, and treated an enemy with
scornful indifference until he attempted to

ride her, when (to use a modern colloquialism) she soon managed to get a bit of her own back.

"Stunsail" another of our ponies, was a good old soul, of worthy character but worthless value.   He had missed his vocation in life, for he ought most certainly to have been a circus pony.   He was full of tricks, not frolicsome or spontaneous ones, but tricks carefully acquired by long hours of practice, such as bowing to ladies, salaaming for bananas, and lying down, pretending to be dead.   It was nice of him to have taken the trouble to acquire these accomplishments, but his fondness for displaying them at all times was often very disturbing to his rider.

Our third pony "John" we always thought a quiet, easy-going individual, until we lent him to a lady who was paying a short visit to Remyo.   She was not an accomplished horse-woman, but would not for the world have confessed to the fact, for she liked to pose as quite fearless, and devoted to riding.

"John's" strong sense of humour first

became apparent in his treatment of her. He soon gauged the extent of the lady's equestrian powers, and enjoyed himself immensely. He did not unseat her or bolt with her : his humour was of a much finer quality ; he merely consistently refused to do anything she wished. When she intended a short ride, "John" would keep her out for hours ; when she was prepared for an afternoon's expedition, " John " would bring her home after a half-mile canter. If she announced her wish to visit her friends at the far side of the station, "John" would take her for a gallop through the jungle ; when she donned her oldest habit to go a quiet country ride "John" would insist upon her calling upon her smartest neighbours, and would walk up to the front door and stand there until she was obliged to dismount and enter.

There was no limit to the mischievous devilry of that pony. When poor Mrs. F. rode out with the rest of the station, her troubles were even greater. When her companions suggested a gallop,

"John" wilfully assumed his slowest walk; and when everyone was riding slowly and conversing pleasantly together, the poor lady would suddenly, without any apparent reason, break off in the middle of a sentence, and set off at the wildest gallop through the jungle, or turn round and ride furiously for home. Nothing would induce her to confess that she could not manage her pony, so she was obliged to invent the wildest excuses and explanations for her conduct. Others thought it was her eccentricity, but we knew it was "John."

CHAPTER XI.

SPORT.

In Burmah the Tiger story takes the place occupied by the fish story in this country, and is stamped, I suspect, with the same unblushing characteristics. Judging from the tiger stories I heard, I could come to no other conclusion than that the Anglo-Indian is possessed of amazing nerve and ingenuity (qualities useful to him alike in the exploit and in the telling of it), and I heard him with ever increasing interest and wonder. The tiger is the favourite theme, though he is but of small account whose chronicle does not also embrace some experiences in the pursuit of the elephant, the bear and other fearful wildfowl indigenous to the country.

Most men own to being a little chary about elephant hunting I found, but our friend the Policeman appeared to have shot them like snipe.   At first I was rather inclined to make light of elephant shooting, they are such exceedingly large animals that I thought even I could hardly fail to bag one if I got him broadside on ; but the Policeman set me right on that point.

From his explanation, I gathered that the elephant is invulnerable save only in one vital part, a spot behind the ear, and the sportsman (according to my narrator) must be as dead on that spot as " Homocea."

My informant also told me terrible stories of how the elephant will turn on his pursuer and trample on him, or tear him in pieces with his tusks, and he gave me further such blood-curdling descriptions of the terrifying noise made by an approaching herd of elephants crashing through the jungle, and trumpeting in their rage, that I felt devoutly thankful that I was visiting this particular district.

The wild elephants of the neighbouring jungle, in their almost human intelligence, recognised the danger to themselves of conduct other than the most retiring and unprovocative character in a locality where the peace was preserved by such an ever threatening Nemesis as our Policeman.

Bears, too, our Policeman had frequently hunted, and many a hair-breadth escape had he effected by running up hill (bears cannot run up hill, you know), or swinging from tree to tree and performing other acrobatic feats which the bear was too heavy to attempt with success.

On one occasion, he said he had been overtaken by the bear, and his left arm chawed in fourteen places (I forget why the bear couldn't be content with one spot and how he protected himself from the animal's further attentions) ; but he didn't mind the bear so much as the well meant efforts of his companion, who, the hero of the episode complained, stood afar off and poured in a devastating fire, directed in a distracted and indiscriminate manner at him and the bear alike. Many and varied indeed were the dangers through which this seemingly fearless hunter had passed unscathed.

Several tigers visited the neighbourhood during my visit, and caused great excitement among the men at the Club, who thought nothing of sitting up all night in an uncomfortable tree, over an unsightly " kill," in hope of compassing the animal's undoing.

Often, alas ! they were doomed to disappointment. On one occasion when my brother and a friend were awaiting a tiger's approach, a mist gathered round them, effectually obscuring everything from their sight. So there they were, obliged, perforce, to sit in darkness, not daring to descend, and of course unable to see, and cheered by listening to the tiger comfortably devouring its prey, within a few yards of their ambush. The Engineer, when he heard this story was for patenting an electric flash light, which could be turned on to light the Sportsman when the tiger was comfortably settled down to his meal, but this original suggestion was

ungratefully rejected, much to his disappointment.

But one afternoon the Thugyi brought
in word that a large tiger had been
marked down in the neighbouring jungle,
and a beat was arranged for the
following day. Then it was that the
Policeman earned our undying gratitude
by proposing that we ladies, who had been
behaving of late in an exemplary manner,
should, for once, be allowed to accompany
the Sportsmen, to see the great sight of
our lives, a tiger shoot.

I doubt whether the suggestion met
with the entire approbation of the other
males, but as the Policeman was organising
the beat, and as we all promised to be very
good and obedient, they agreed reluctantly
to take us. Women, perhaps naturally, are
considered very much "de trop" on these
occasions. A tiger shoot is a serious,
sometimes a dangerous business, and
female frivolities and nerves would deci-
dedly be embarrassments.

I heard a story of a girl, reputed to be a
great Sportswoman and a good shot, who

accompanied her male friends upon one of these expeditions. Platforms had been built for the Sportsmen in the trees in the line of the beat, and she shared one with a man who was more accustomed to shooting and hunting than to the society of the other sex, whom he held in much greater awe than any wild animal, however dangerous. When the tiger made its appearance, the girl promptly fainted, and her poor companion spent a most unhappy ten minutes between the unconscious girl and the enraged tiger, being far more alarmed at the former.

However, to return to my story, when we had given assurances that we never fainted, nor had hysterics, nor grew tired; and had promised faithfully not to move a muscle, not to speak a single word, not to disobey an order, and above all not to want to shoot, the men folk graciously allowed us to accompany them; but it was not to create a precedent.

How excited we were and how nervous! A seat in a tree did not appear to me to offer much security against the tiger's attack, however high it might be. Tigers, I had always been told, are near relations to cats, and I knew cats climb trees. When I nervously breathed these doubts to the Policeman, he solemnly assured me that tigers will not climb, and by standing on their hind legs can only reach up about fourteen feet ; but this did not convince me, for had I not seen in my nursery days (and early impressions are lasting ones) brilliantly coloured pictures of tiger shoots wherein the tiger was invariably depicted, leaping into the air, or climbing fiercely up the side of an elephant, while the nervous occupant of the howdah peered cautiously over the edge ? Was I to ignore the lessons of my youth ? I can only explain this inconsistency by suggesting that tigers may have changed their habits with the advance of civilization.

Nothing was talked of that evening but tigers and tiger shooting. The Policeman and other local sportsmen were in great request, and their stories were listened to with an interest and belief which I should think quite astonished them. Even to the village did the excitement spread, for the love of sport is as prevalent among the Burmans as among Englishmen ; and the natives are well paid for serving as beaters.

Early in the morning the hunting party assembled in our compound, and, after partaking of a cheery " chota hazri," we set out, a merry cavalcade consisting of seven men, and three women, and accompanied by a miscellaneous collection of servants and native " shikarries."

It was one of those fresh, cool, delicious mornings that make one feel inclined to sing with Pippa :

" The morning's at seven, The hillside's dew pearled."
" God's in His Heaven, all's well with the World."

In spite of qualms regarding the ordeal before us, we enjoyed that early ride, and were a very happy, hungry crew when we arrived at the jungle village whither breakfast had already been despatched. We found everything ready, prepared by the Club Khansamah, and his staff of silent, well-trained loogalays, and we breakfasted in the "hpoongyi kyaung" itself, surrounded by images of Gaudama, by sacred

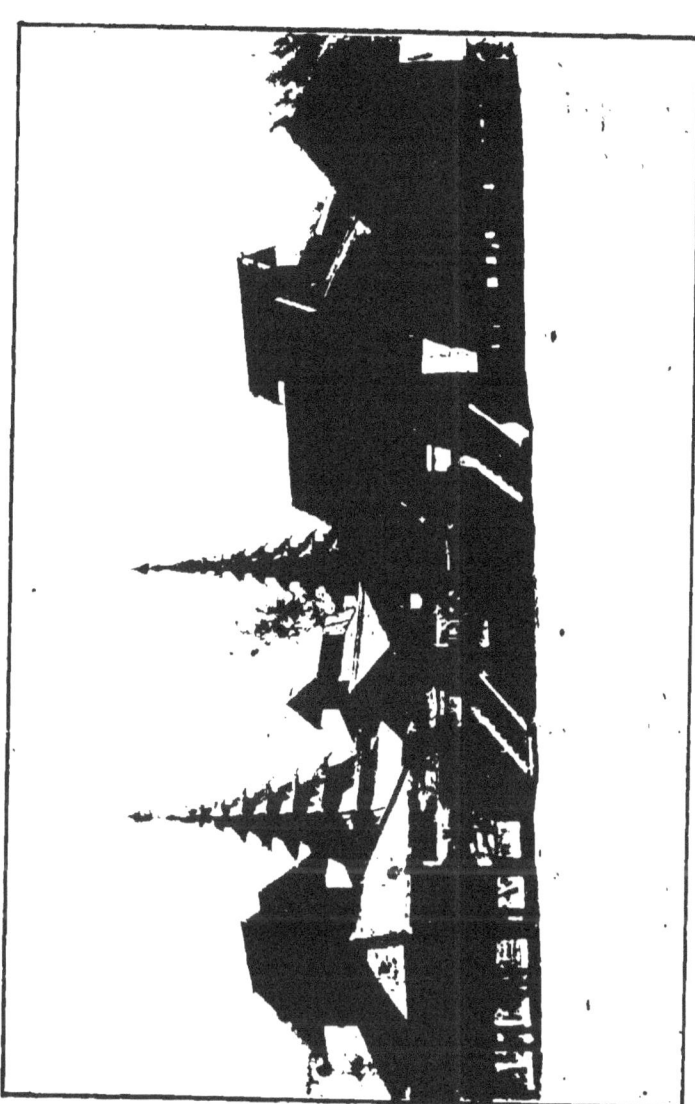

A HPOONGYI KYAUNG MONASTERY

pictures and bells ; shaded by lovely groups of bamboos, and watched from afar by an interested crowd of young Burmans, whose shaven heads and yellow robes showed them to be the hpoongyi's pupils.

But we were not allowed to linger too long in idleness, discussing the merits of "the chicken and ham, the muffin and toast, and the strawberry jam," to say nothing of luscious pineapples, incomparable bananas (differing as much from the banana we meet in England, as chalk from cheese), the much vaunted mangostines, the objectionable (from my way of thinking) custard apple, and the hundred other delicacies which our generous hosts had provided for our delectation. I had scarcely exchanged three words with the pineapples, and had only a bowing acquaintance with the plum cake, when the doughty Policeman gave the word to start.

It was really extraordinary how the presence of danger and responsibility affected the bearing of our Policeman. The change came on quite suddenly, in the middle of breakfast, and was maintained

o

till evening. He was transformed from a jovial, talkative personage, to one sombre and morose, refusing to utter a word more than was absolutely necessary, greeting all observations with a discouraging frown or a shake of the head, and, in all his movements and actions displaying the impressive characteristics of "Hawk-eye," and other Indian Hunter friends of one's youth. We ladies were immensely impressed, and did our best to imitate his severe expression and noiseless, stalking gait, as closely as possible. Perhaps we presented rather a weird appearance, steal-ing along with harassed, stern set faces, and cautious steps, like stage pirates, but concluding that it was the proper rôle to adopt on such an occasion we adopted it.

Outside the kyaung we met the beaters; a picturesque group in their bright coloured dresses, armed with sticks, cans, whistles, and everything sufficiently noisy to rouse "Shere Khan" from his noonday sleep. These beaters were despatched, under the direction of a native "shikarrie," to com-mence their work about half-a-mile to the westward, while we went to take up our position to the east of the rumoured position of the tiger.

By this time the sun was up, and it was becoming very hot. For about half an hour we stole along in single file through the jungle. Half the men went before us to part the tangled bushes, the remainder brought up the rear, lest one of us should be lost ; a possible and very unpleasant prospect in jungle so thick that it is impossible to see a yard around. We were very silent, partly from excitement, partly because silence was advisable ; for who could tell what sleeping inhabitant of the jungle we might pass within a few yards.

At last our leader judged that we had penetrated far enough ; he halted the party, and assigned to each gun its position. We ladies were each confided to the care of a good shot, and repaired with our respective protectors to the trees appointed for us by our leader. After some original research into the difficulties of tree climbing (especially tree climbing when the tree has no branches within five or six feet of the ground), and the unpleasant sensation of missing one's footing and slithering down the trunk,—I at length, with the aid of much pulling, pushing, and other forcible assistance from my companion, attained my perch, and my protector climbed to a position in a tree close to mine. We had no platform to sit upon, but perched on the most convenient branches available. A branch of a tree is not the most comfortable seat in the world, and before the day was over I had ceased to envy "the birds of the air, who make their habitations among the branches."

After all the sportsmen were settled in their relative positions, about a hundred yards apart, a weary time of waiting ensued. No one spoke. Everywhere around us were the mysterious humming, rustling sounds of the jungle, and far away to the westward we heard the faint noise of shouting and belaboured "tom-toms," which told us that the beaters had commenced their work. The strain of excitement was terrible.

I measured the distance between my feet and the ground, and calculated that, my tree not being very high, the tiger would experience little difficulty in reaching me. I mechanically drew up my feet, and tightened my hold on my sun umbrella ; I remembered my board ship companions had assured me that poking an animal in the eye is very effective, but I didn't feel much confidence in this advice. Nor did I feel much confidence in my oft-tried, and much vaunted presence of mind ; absence of body would have comforted me more. I peered up among the branches, and decided where I would place my feet if a sudden flight to higher regions should be necessary. Then I came to the conclusion that I didn't like tiger shooting at all.

I glanced at my protector ; he looked cool and alert. He was one of those men who appear absolutely uninterested in all that is going on until the supreme moment arrives, when they wake up suddenly and distinguish themselves, after which they relapse again into their former indifference. I regained my courage at sight of his coolness, and listened.

Intense stillness around and behind us ; even the jungle had ceased to whisper. Everything seemed waiting in eager expectancy. But, before us, drawing ever nearer and nearer, were the beaters, rattling sticks and cans, whistling, shouting, and playing on "tom-toms," while between them and us, aroused from its heavy sleep, slinking away from the noise and disturbance was————what ? The possibilities of a jungle drive are end-less. Suddenly the high grass beneath my tree parted, "Now for it," I think. But no ! it is only a gyee, hurrying away with scared eyes from the unknown danger behind. It may escape to-day ; its enemy, man, is after bigger game.

Ever nearer drew the beaters. "Will it never end ? " I whisper. But what was that ? A loud report close to my ear ; something flashes past in the grass below, there is a loud roar of pain and fury, and then "all is over except the shouting."

For a few moments we waited in astonishment that it is all over so quickly, and in doubt if the animal be really dead.

Then everyone tumbled simultaneously from their perches and hurried to the spot.

There lay the tiger, quite dead, but looking so lifelike that while I put my hand in his mouth or felt his cruel claws, I was conscious of a half fear lest he should be only shamming, and should come to life again with a sudden spring. The beautiful skin was uninjured, save where the bullet had entered the spine, and as we looked at him, the very emblem of strength and beauty lying there, slain without even a fight for life, I think we all felt a little pity.

But pity soon gave way to triumph. The beaters arrived and crowded round the tiger, laughing and chattering ; mocking the animal which had held them in such terror while he lived, and trying to steal his whiskers, which the Burmans value as charms.

But we soon found we were hot, thirsty, and tired, so we set out on our return journey to Remyo, the beaters carrying our victim in triumph fastened on a long bamboo. News of our success had preceded us, and as we approached the village we were met by an immense crowd of admiring natives, in that condition of giggling and jabbering excitement to which only a crowd composed largely of Madrassees can attain. So persistent were the attacks made upon the tiger's whiskers, that it became necessary at last to tie his head up in a bag, and in that undignified condition he was borne home and deposited safely in the club compound, where during the day, he was visited and admired by every inhabitant of the station.

Thus ended my first and only tiger shoot. How I wish I could electrify my readers with descriptions of expeditions wherein I myself would appear as the heroine, shooting tigers, and performing other moving exploits by flood and field. But it may not be. The eager search after truth which has been so noticeable lately among the British public, restrains such interesting flights of fancy, and in these days, romancers who would display their quality to an appreciative audience, must address themselves to the Marines, or to the British Association.

There is endless variety of game in the neighbourhood of Remyo. Snipe are almost as common as sparrows at home; partridges, peacocks, jungle fowl, gyee, and hares all abound, and many an enjoyable shooting expedition is undertaken, sometimes with, sometimes without the excuse of "business" in the district.

Well provided with ammunition, food, drink, rugs, and bedding, the Anglo Indian sets out for two or three days sport, wandering from place to place, sleeping in the open sided "zayats," near the hpoongyi kyaungs, and spending the day in the jungle, in eager search after the Englishman's great desire "something to kill."

Some of the native "shikarries" who accompany these expeditions are splendid men. They are very silent, very uninterested in, even contemptuous of, things not connected with sport, but devoted to their profession, and as keenly excited, as delighted at success, or disappointed at failure, as any good sportsman all the world over ; and possessing moreover a knowledge of the habits and customs of the jungle folk scarcely surpassed by " Mowgli " himself.

A form of sport much indulged in by the Shan chiefs in the past, but which has been strenuously discouraged was "Collecting Heads." The last exponent of the game dwelt in the hills on the Shan State border, and was the hereditary leader of a large tribe of men as fierce and savage as himself. He was an ancient chief, proud of his race, his power, and position ; proud too of his home, and above all proud of his wonderful bodily strength. Many and marvellous are the stories told of his extraordinary doings. On one occasion, unarmed, he fought and killed a tiger, clinging to its throat until he throttled it. He bore the marks of the contest, huge scars upon his head, and throat, and chest, until his dying day.

It was his custom (as doubtless it had been the custom of his ancestors, and of many of their neighbours) to descend periodically from his mountain heights alone and spend a few weeks in the neigh-

bouring plains, engaged in his favourite
hobby of collecting heads. He was not
particular what heads he collected, but he
preferred human ones when he could get
them. He would remain in the plains for
a while, way-laying, hunting, and slaying
as many of his fellow creatures as he could
meet with (occasionally perhaps varying
the sport by killing a tiger) and at last when
he grew for the nonce weary of this amusement, he would return in triumph to his
tribe, and display to their admiring gaze
his ghastly spoils.

The placid native suffered his hostile
inroads with that fatalism with which they
regard all misfortune. But one day the
Chief made a slight mistake by adding to
his collection the head of an Englishman
(who was no doubt poaching in the Chief's
country) and for this departure from the
accepted rules of the game, he paid penalty.

A detachment of soldiers was despatched,
who soon scattered the tribe and captured
the offender. I met the subaltern who had
been in charge of the escort, which brought
him down to the plains, and he described

to me the desperate efforts the fierce old man made to escape. He was bound hand and foot, watched night and day by four men, and his bonds were inspected every hour ; on one of these inspections it was discovered that the ropes were frayed and gnawed half away. But his efforts were of no avail ; though he had the strength of a giant he could do nothing against such overpowering odds.

When at length they reached the plains, he turned to have a last look at the vanishing shadows of the hills, which no doubt he had loved with that silent, passionate love felt for their home by the inhabitants of all mountainous countries, and after a final desperate effort to kill himself, he suddenly seemed to relinquish all hope, and resigned himself stolidly to his fate.

His defiance and strength seemed to pass away with that last sight of his beloved hills, and a broken-spirited, weak, helpless, old man was all that remained. They brought him to Rangoon and banished his old, worn-out body to the Andaman Islands, but his proud, fierce spirit fled back with that last look at the hills, and haunts the wild regions where he loved to roam.

CHAPTER XII.

—

THE RETURN.

—

"But that's all shove be'ind me—long ago and fur away
An' there ain't no busses runnin' from the Bank to Mandalay."

"For the temple-bells are callin', and it's there that I would be
By the old Moulmein Pagoda, looking lazy at the sea."

(Kipling.)

—

To the stranger in this fascinating country, days are as minutes, months as days, and it seemed that scarcely had I arrived and commenced to look around me, when my visit came to an end, and sadly bidding farewell to Remyo and its many delights, all too soon I had to return home.

Alas! too, I found I was compelled to renew my acquaintance with the Burmese pony, the only alternative being a bullock cart ; and let those who have ridden forty miles along an up-country road in a Burmese bullock cart —— but no ! I do not like to think such an experience can have befallen my worst enemy.

Once more, therefore, I mounted to the saddle, and rode, or more properly speaking bumped, twenty miles the first day. At the end of that distance I had no desire to proceed further, nor, I am sure, had the pony. Accordingly, we stopped at the now familiar dâk bungalow, and stabled ourselves and our ponies for the night. I do not know what were my pony's feelings that night as he thought over the events of the day, but they cannot have been pleasant. He was a strong-minded pony (possibly he had some sympathy for his rider) and having come to the conclusion that a repetition on the morrow of the past day's proceedings would be unpleasant and unwise, during the night he slipped his halter and gently trotted back to Remyo, accompanied by my brother's and the orderly's mounts.

When we arose in the morning, all we found in the little hut at the bottom of the bungalow compound were three belated looking saddles and some broken bridle reins, and the only course open to us was to continue our journey on foot.

Some people, I believe, pretend to see humour in such situations, but we were not amused. The heat was awful, the road almost knee deep in dust, and as we plodded along for several miles, losing our way in short cuts, scrambling down precipitous ravines and dry water courses, and exchanging no single word, but keeping all our breath for the exertion of clambering out again, I became, by comparison, almost reconciled to the previous day's experiences.

When at last we reached the foot of the hills, and found a "gharry" waiting to convey us to Mandalay, we resembled pillars of dust, and were as thirsty as the desert. I was so tired that I forgot to be sentimental over the last glimpse of the hills; and as we approached Mandalay, beautiful in her bower of green, with the sun shining as ever on the "dreaming spires," the white pagodas, and the golden domes, my one and only desire was "Drink."

I had delayed my departure from Remyo as late as possible in the hopes of witnessing a "hpoongyi burning," one of the most characteristic Burmese festivals. The holy man had died some time previously, and in order to do his memory due honour, his body had been preserved many months, and the burning, with the many strange rites and festivities which invariably accompany such ceremonies, was announced to take place the week before my departure. But from some unknown cause (perhaps they discovered he had been more virtuous than they at first imagined) the authorities suddenly decided to preserve the body until a more imposing pageant could be prepared, so I missed the sight; and having delayed my departure, 1 had time only to spend a few hours in Mandalay and Rangoon before embarking on the homeward bound steamer.

It was very sad, that departure from Rangoon, where so many friends were left behind, as the last beauties of this bewitching country faded slowly from sight. The glaring noonday sunshine shed no illusory haze over the scene. The

P

muddy brown water of the river and the ugly shores lined with factories and mills, seemed a foretaste of the matter-of-fact land to which we were returning; but behind rose the distant palm trees, and the golden dome; and the soft music of the tinkling bells of the pagoda, bidding us a last farewell, was wafted to us by the perfume laden eastern breeze.

My homeward voyage was without any extraordinary incident, and in due course I arrived at Marseilles. This well-known port requires no description, but I must say a few words in its favour; it is so universally disparaged.

The noisy, unsavoury Marseilles of the docks and harbour is very different from Marseilles viewed from that magnificent church, "Notre Dame de la garde." When we climb to the summit of the rock whereon stands the stately white church, surmounted by the huge golden image of the Virgin, keeping watch over the ships that enter the harbour, and shining as a beacon miles out to sea, a welcome sight to the longing eyes of the

home coming sailor ; when we look down
from our height over the pretty little red
and white houses, the graceful spires, and
the clusters of dark green foliage nestling
in the shelter of the high white cliffs which
enclose the harbour ; and again beyond the
town, beyond the rugged brown rocks,
and the placid deep blue water, to the
ancient " Chateau D'If," dark and forbid-
ding in the midst of the sunny landscape,
we acknowledge that nature in the
bestowal of her beauties has not, after
all, confined her gifts to the dreaming East.

I think the true reason why Marseilles
is so frequently spoken of with disfavour is
on account of the " Bouillabaisse," the
terrible mixture which delights the palates
of the natives, and which innocent
strangers are induced to partake of under
the delusion that it must therefore be good
for human food.

The only recommendation this dish possesses is the curious interest it arouses in
one's mind as to what it is really composed of.
One never knows what form of fish, flesh,
or _bad_ red herring one may encounter

next. The appearance of the dish re-
sembles one's childish imaginations of a
" Mess of Pottage." Its scent suggests
Marseilles harbour, and the stoke hole of a
Channel steamer. I myself was never
sufficiently enterprising to taste it, but
judging by the expression of haggard
thought that overspread the features of
some who were so venturesome, I should
say the taste must be " mystic, wonderful," and that years of careful study are
necessary to attain to a true appreciation
of its subtle delicacy.

I think the journey from Marseilles to
London is the most wearisome that can be
undertaken. After the warmth, the quiet,
and the absence of hurry to which I had
become accustomed in the East, I found
the bustle and noise, added to the piercing
cold of a European April, almost overpowering. I shivered on deck, as our
steamer ploughed her way across the
Channel, through a damp clinging fog,
and when at last the welcome white cliffs
came into sight, I was far too miserable to
wax sentimental over this return to my

native shore, and I longed only for tea and a fire.

Yet after all, despite the contrast betwixt sunshine and yellow fog, between jungle glades and London streets, despite all the advantages which we know that every other clime and country can boast over our own, England is England still, and Home is Home.

And now let me offer a word of advice to those who, like myself, undertake adventurous wanderings far from their native land, and recount the same with many embellishments. On their return home, let them beware of introducing to the admiring circle of their friends, any who may have accompanied them on their travels.

I had been back at home some three months, had told my story, and had established my reputation, when one day a visitor from Burmah arrived.

He had not been long in the house before some uncalled-for allusion was made to the historic occasion on which I defended my sister's house in Remyo from a body of dacoits. He denied all knowledge of the incident. Suspicions awoke in the breasts of my friends. They questioned the visitor about my struggle with the tiger, my adventure with the bear, my heroic bravery on the occasion of the shipwreck, and about all my other best inspired narrations.

Alas! he denied them all, and my credit was gone for ever. I fancy some have even ceased to believe that I have been to Burmah at all, and some have become so suspicious as to make enquiries as to whether I really am myself. It is hard! and the recently notorious contributor to the "Wide Wide World" Magazine has my deep sympathy. Would I had lived in the days of Columbus; I would have discovered more than America, had I enjoyed such excellent opportunities as did he.

*　　*　　*　　*　　*

Thus ends the account of my experiences in Burmah, and of the impression left on my mind by this oft-described country.

Perhaps distance lends enchantment to the view, and makes me forget the evils of the climate, the dangers and discomforts of life there, the slowness of locomotion, the lack of many so-called benefits of civilisation ; and I seem to remember only a land where the sun is always shining and the world is always gay ; where the air is heavy with delicious eastern scents, and filled with the harmonious music of the temple bells, as they are gently swayed by the whispering breeze. A land where the hues of earth can vie with the brilliancy of the sunset, and the eye is feasted with delicately blended colours.

Here Beauty and Peace hold eternal honeymoon. Misery seems to have no place in this land of delight, but contentment ever reigns, and the happy Burman dreams away his life in a paradise of sunshine. No one who has visited this country can ever forget it, but learns to understand too well that fascination so well expressed by Mr. Kipling : " If you've 'eard the East a' callin', you won't never 'eed nought else."

I remember Burmah, too, as a land of picturesque buildings, of rich jewels, exquisite costumes, and beautiful graceful women. A land of kindly hearts, friendly welcomes, and ungrudging hospitality.

These are remembered when the last glint of the golden-domed pagoda has faded into the shadowy distance, and we sail away from the peaceful sunshine and the palm trees, westward ho! to this hurrying, bustling modern world, where, though beauty exists, we have no time to appreciate it, and where, like King Midas of old, we would turn all we touch to glittering gold, and for ever destroy its charm.

R. PLATT, PRINTER, WIGAN.

www.ingramcontent.com/pod-product-compliance
Lightning Source LLC
Chambersburg PA
CBHW020353030726
47496CB00007B/2125